W9-CLJ-945

An Irish Eye

G·K Hall &Cº.

This Large Print Book carries the
Seal of Approval of N.A.V.H.

An Irish Eye

John Hawkes

G.K. Hall & Co.
Thorndike, Maine

Copyright © John Hawkes, 1997

All rights reserved.

Published in 1998 by arrangement with Viking Penguin,
a member of Penguin Putnam Inc.

G.K. Hall Large Print Core Collection.

The text of this Large Print edition is unabridged.
Other aspects of the book may vary from the original edition.

Set in 18 pt. Plantin by Juanita Macdonald.

Printed in the United States on permanent paper.

**Library of Congress Catalog Card Number: 97-94771
ISBN: 0-7838-8380-3 (lg. print : hc)**

For Sophie

And for my editor,
Mark Stafford

Author's Note

My thanks to Patrick McGrath for giving me Moira Moylan, Finnula Malloy, Shivaughn Breheny, Molly O'Malley, and Dervla O'Shannon herself.

I am a foundling.

But in point of truth, is there an Irish girl who is not? Let her just have a loving mummy and daddo and papers and name to prove who she is as testified by the parish priest, and a bed in which no one ever slept before her and stories told her by her mummy and daddo — still she is a foundling, I say, for she cannot be sure of her parentage, kisses on her tender cheek or not. Of course the lads are exempt. The lads are sons of this angry land of ours, and there's an end to it. But just let a person be a female and she's a foundling, to one degree or another, even if she's got a shiny pram to carry her off to Mass in. Better to have done with it all and be the real thing, as I am, and you could not have a more proper foundling than me, as Foundling Mother can verify herself, since it was she who took me in and herself who lifted me in a scrap of blanket from that same frail basket left in doorways down the ages.

Take care of her, said the note pinned to my scrap of blanket. *She's a good girl.*

And that I am and that's who I am with no questions asked. Foundling Mother says she called me Thistle because she knew as soon as she picked me up that I was to be as skinny and prickly and unwanted all my life as any thistle growing in the country round. From the start I clung to Foundling Mother's skirts and begged her to tell me such things. She never tired of me dragging on her skirts or of all my little sisters doing the same, though in truth our older girls, keeping in mind that we ranged from only days out of the basket to twenty-something years in age, often swept up the smaller girls and invented things to tell them, thus giving Foundling Mother a time to catch her breath, poor thing. Yet was there ever a woman less grudging than herself, no matter how we swarmed on her, laughing and clutching her person and demanding she sing to us or begging her to teach us what she knew? There was not. There was not a certified mum in all this proud little country of ours as selfless and generous and blessed with humor as Foundling Mother. I'll attest to that, as will so many more dead or alive.

I am well aware of the dark things said, the accusations of little girls worked to death and starved and allowed to go for weeks on end unwashed and shivering in the cold, and aware of the whippings and neglect to the point of illness and running away, and all because of the greed and meanness of the spinsters put in charge of the likes of us. And I have heard that there are those who say that foundlings deserve no better, castaways and charity cases that we really are. Foundling Mother! Protect us from shameful politicians and spiteful citizens. But Foundling Mother! I am loath to believe that anyone could spread such ill-feeling about my kind and the sweet women who are mothers as no ordinary women are.

In the dark of night the dormitory

smelled of blood and stiffly laundered sheets, of the comfort of thirty girls or more who had each other, the occasional new arrival being in separate quarters and under Foundling Mother's personal care. Undeniably there were sounds of fitful weeping or fearful cries in the darkness, but the smaller girls were never left for long to suffer what they could not help, and soon enough the older girls had restored peace to our sleep.

Naturally the daylight hours in the Foundling Home, or Saint Martha's as was its formal name, since anything of a profound nature must be kept under the church's wing, quickened all our spirits as the night could not. There was the kitchen presided over by Foundling Mother herself, usually with an infant on one or both hips and perspiration shining on her lovely face, and in that darkly tiled room we hefted iron pots as large as ourselves, dropping them sometimes, stew and all, to great cries of dismay, and learned to stand at one or the other of the great black stoves and how to avoid burning our fingers or arms on that hot iron. Irish stew, whether made of bits of mutton or stringy beef and baskets of potatoes as large as our babies' heads, was what we most loved to cook and loved to eat, though the various soups concocted by Foundling Mother and as thick as porridge satisfied our cravings nearly as well. Oh, the glorious smells that filled our kitchen and arose even from our pails of slops! And the greasy pots, the plates piled up in the sinks, the reluctant suds, the scalding water and our arms plunged in so deep we were wet to the shoulders, and just as sopping wet was our hair that hung in our faces. All about us the wall tiles were a fading white and running with cracks, they were that old, and the spigots on the old soapstone sinks were brass as green as the lichen on the open country where we were not permitted except under the strictest supervision and where my bristly namesake grew. The floors in that kitchen were of tiles as dark as stone and polished smooth by generations of industrious foundlings, young and old, who found that in cooking and doing the scullery work they could best imitate the grown women they would become.

Floor's wet, girls. Don't slip and fall!

Our dining room offered not much diversion, though twice a day, since we only ate two meals a day, those of us scheduled to serve the others that month had the pleasure of carrying in the trays, a task requiring serious knitting of the brows and concentration, and of chopping up the crusty loaves baked under the all-wise eyes and nose of Foundling Mother, herself long hours before the dawning of the day in question. Teams of us rotated at the baking, though there was no such relief for Foundling Mother. Seven days a week there was the baking of the dough, work that exhausted the best of us, and the staggering heat of the ovens and the smells that turned many a child's head in her sleep.

Mother in heaven, bless this humble fare. Amen.

The laundry room, now, was nearly as wondrous a place as the kitchen, and as dangerous. The heaps of little garments with their various stains were in themselves startling to the mind, bereft as they were of the bodies they had so recently covered, all these bits of clothing collapsed and deflated and haphazard in piles that made me think of dead children or small girls missing in some sort of mysterious naked flight over the forbidden country round. And oh, the vats and tubs into which we flung these remnants as of some terrible slaughter that had never occurred but made us shiver all the same, and the wooden paddles with which we pushed and beat our sisters' clothes in water smelling of some dread chemical and burning our nostrils. While outside, beyond the grated

15

windows above our heads, for the laundry was in the basement of the Foundling Home, crows sang as best they could and washed themselves in the rain — oh, to take one's turn in the laundry was real work. The water we used was boiled in iron boilers and steaming when it entered the tubs and vats, and many a careless girl blistered an entire underside of a little forearm and staggered off in tears in search of her Foundling Mother.

I need not say much about our showering save that thirty naked girls of all ages laughing and screaming and slipping about with their glistening bodies and hanks of hair drenched under the jets of cold water brought even the shyest among us to appreciation. Twice a week we scrubbed ourselves and each other, while certain girls chased other girls in and out and among the bathing rest of us.

Behave yourselves! Behave, you wayward things!

Beyond our routine satisfactions were the special pleasures. On the last Sunday midday meal of the month, for instance, we feasted on great platters of sausage made by Foundling Mother herself and heaps of bacon cut in slices as thick as my little finger, and mounds of boiled potatoes, all of it washed down with pitchers of beer in portions appropriate for girls of all ages. What a cry went up when that steaming fare was carried in to our tables.

Then too we had our sports like the best of them, and in boots and ill-fitting socks and tops and shorts donated by the administration of Saint

George's, the local school for boys who were the elite of Ireland and who never once came up to see us play, we charged back and forth over our pocked and weed-tufted field at our football, shouting and getting flushed of face and tearing each other's clothing and bruising each other's shins, thanks to the boots that were inevitably too large and smelling of the boy's feet they had once protected, so that we kicked each other with the maleness of those boys too proud to watch the foundlings flying and making goals, though we were excellent at that rough game, as I don't mind saying. And dramatics? Of course we had our dramatics in the dining hall, with the tables pushed to the side and Foundling Mother as coach and central member of the audience, the little ones weeping and cowering whenever we acted our dragons and hunters and various demons of the forest.

We were by no means confined to Saint Martha's on the hill, since our Foundling Home was in fact an old brick building built before memory atop one of two hills that rose from opposite ends of the little metropolis that lay below and between them, though mainly we ventured forth in coats and bonnets to troop down the incline and through the near-empty streets to attend the earliest possible Mass three mornings a week and on certain feast days that fell throughout the year. Yes, the earliest Mass when the church was darkest and coldest and least attended. Foundling Mother herded us to the rear of the chancel, where she tried to minimize the presence of her thirty girls, which gives a certain credence to the theory that foundlings may not generally be wanted, even in church. There was not a girl among us who suspected any such thing, however, and who was not enraptured by the golden figures we could not see for the darkness and by the smells of wax and piety and especially by the sight of priest and acolytes, man and boys after all, whose glory was shared to a lesser degree by all Ireland's men and boys, which is not to be irreverent despite the sanctity that breathed on that priest and boys up there at the altar. We foundlings were not invited to that selfsame altar until after the scattering of true parishioners had gone about their morning business. When we left the church, savoring one and all its mystery, and began our ragged marching back up to that dour brick building that was our home, there were always a few hoots and hellos called out to us from the passing crowds more in good humor than mockery, as it seemed to me.

It is true that from the outside the Foundling Home was not an attractive sight, with its severe boxlike shape and weather-darkened brick, and on the windows, the rusted iron grates intended not to confine us, as I have already implied, but to protect us, though from what or whom no one could say. After all, and no matter that Saint Martha's was one of three public institutions for the good of the people, there was neither a prison nor a mental asylum anywhere in the vicinity, and where else might we find the kind of person obsessed with doing harm to foundlings?

At any rate the three public institutions of the little metropolis of Carrickfergus, which was the name of the place, included our own Saint Martha's, then, plus a hospital, and on the opposite hill from ours, the Old Soldiers' Home, of which we shall have much more, thanks to a remarkable scheme conceived on the spur of the moment one afternoon by its director. In its forbidding aspects the Old Soldiers' Home could not have more resembled the Foundling Home of Carrickfergus, brick and square shape and grated windows and all, the only difference between the two being that the inmates of the one were girls and of the other, old men. Thus there was an inevitable attraction reaching out from Saint Martha's to Saint Clement's, as the Old Soldiers' Home was formally known. As for the hospital, its name was Saint Claire's, while that of the school for proud boys was Saint George's. So the little metropolis of Carrickfergus was a town of saints, as we might say, which was to the good of us all.

If I have given the impression that there was only one adult woman and thirty girls living in Saint Martha's, or that no men or boys ever appeared in our midst or that nothing untoward ever happened in the Foundling Home that faced the Old Soldiers' Home across the metropolis lying wet and smoky between them, then I must correct such an impression, though I was anything but a pedantic girl whose penchant for exactitude gives her only a straight back and a drying up of the fluids. Quite the opposite. I was tall for my weight and quick to exercise my mind. But I followed my flesh, thin though I was and once I had gotten the first impulse and the knack of it, and I shall never in my life be borne down by the mere truth of things. That said, I must confess that Foundling Mother was not by her single self the mother of us all but had for companion, assistant, sister in lovingness if you will, Mrs. Jencks, who was always there and ready to obtrude from behind the scenes when Foundling Mother was finally too tired, if that may be imagined, and simply too distracted by it all, too overcome by the demands of stove and ovens and lessons and consoling, with her clear eye losing focus and a strand of hair come

loose and hanging down on her fore-
head, to carry on. Here I must add
that if Foundling Mother was in a
sense the true mother of us all, the
woman to whom we turned as if she
had in fact borne us all, nonetheless
it was Mrs. Jencks who from her own
full bosom gave warm mother's milk
to the littlest girl, from the day or night
of arrival until she was large enough
to eat what the rest of us ate from plate
or bowl.

No matter what I have said about
the difficulty of the work that had to
be done in the laundry, with its steam
and burns and smarting of the eyes,
the hardest and least interesting work
was to be found in scrubbing the
floors. Can you see half a dozen girls
of various ages down on their hands
and knees on the cold tiles with their

skirts hiked up and pushing buckets and sponges before them, reddening their poor bare knees with no relief in sight, since the end of the dark corridor in question proceeded into the darkness much farther than the eye could see? Well, that was a dreary business, as I can tell you from personal experience too unpleasant and too extensive to recount.

Foundling Mother, who never went by her ordinary name, which was Mrs. Jennings, though the Mrs. was just a matter of form or courtesy since the dear woman was never married a day in her life, was herself reputed to have arrived at Saint Martha's in a basket left at our door one snowy night, and so to have grown from foundling girl to Foundling Mother knowing more than any woman could what lay in store for her charges and how best to train them and succor them, though not a drop of mother's milk came from her bosom. Not only did she hold us close to her own warmth, and cook for us or at least supervise the cooking, and shed her benevolence and personal knowledge on the way things went in Saint Martha's, but it was she who gave a name to every one of the foundlings who were children of that home at any one time, give or take a few. She loved names and loved naming us, so that in my day we had a Moira Moylan and a Finnula Malloy and a Shivaughn Breheny and a Molly O'Malley and a Dervla O'Shannon, who was myself though Thistle was how I had been called from the beginning, as I have said. She chose our names as if she were some sort of living compendium of the most florid of all female names extant in the annals of Ireland's red-haired women. We had our share of red-haired girls, from the palest strawberry to the darkest shades of blood from a wound, and freckled to one extent or another from faint to blatant, though sorry to say I was not one of them, having dullish dark hair somewhere between black and brown and not a single freckle on my cheeks or flat chest. Sometimes I wished that I could go by my official name, since I did thrill to the sound of Dervla, which was a good indication of the way I was without looking the part.

Once I happened to be passing Foundling Mother's rooms when the door stood open and a silence like the end of the world came from within.

And what did I see but the woman who was our one and only mother gripping little Moira Moylan about the waist and holding up the child's skirts and with a bit of stick whipping the child's bottom, without a sound as I say. I stopped, of course, and Foundling Mother raised her smiling face in my direction, while continuing on with the whipping.

I found her going through my things, dear. And we cannot have that, can we?

But we must remember that Foundling Mother worked for us and with us, maintaining order among her thirty or so daughters, as she called us, and supervising the seamstress down in Carrickfergus, the widow who made by hand but only to three standard sizes and not according to our needs the dark blue dresses that were the familiar uniform of Saint Martha's. Shoes were a problem, since these could not be made by a cobbler exclusively for us, but arrived in boxes as a gift of charity, besought of course by Foundling Mother, who arranged not only that we had shoes on our feet but musical instruments to play in our marching band. For indeed we had a very lively marching band with half a dozen girls at trumpets and trombones and *Saint Martha's Home for Foundling Girls* painted in a lovely green on the sides of the bass drum, which I myself beat proudly to a grand rhythm. We caused quite a stir when we went marching at the end of the parade in a wonderful rain down the streets of Carrickfergus to the shouts of the admiring crowd.

But shoes, as I say, were a problem, since they came to us in hefty boxes of mismatched parts and a jumble of sizes, so that many a one of us walked with a limp and one of her feet turned in, which is no doubt why we preferred going about in our bare feet, as we often did.

Remember, I mean to correct the impression I may have given that nothing untoward ever happened at Saint Martha's, so that here I will mention an incident that comes to mind perhaps because of the thought of deformity, of which we had our share in fears and bodies. So did Mr. Bailey the butcher's boy, a frail little thing with a sallow face and a gimp leg, who on the designated afternoon delivered our meager ration of red meat through the rear door that led to the kitchen. Other boys came to us, of course, since there was Joe Dan's own son who brought us fish and Padder Casey the greengrocer's lad who brought heaps of fresh vegetables as ordered by Foundling Mother. But of these young creatures only Mr. Bailey the butcher's boy whose name was Red Eddie, carried himself about on a gimp leg of which he was sorely ashamed.

Again I remember silence throughout our rooms and corridors, the foundlings other than me being on their knees for midday prayer or out in our stubbly field kicking each other. It was a kind day in spring, with windows open behind the grates and the smell of clouds and fledgling birds coming in on the breeze. All at once I heard a shout or cry of a boy's voice that made me perk up my head, I can tell you.

I won't! I won't! I don't want to!

So naturally I went off in search of that voice and found it soon enough, and saw that it belonged to Red Eddie who, of all things, was in our otherwise empty kitchen and lying beneath one of the massive tables there and, further, was struggling beneath Finnula Malloy, no less, who, that hefty girl of ten or twelve years of age, was holding down poor Red Eddie by the sheer weight of her. No sound came from that grappling pair except when Mr. Bailey the butcher's boy managed to twist away his head and repeat his little cry that no one heard, except of course for me and Finnula Malloy. It was a plaintive pathetic sound since obviously Red Eddie was suffering greatly and was no match at all for Finnula.

I won't! I won't! I don't want to!

What was there for me to do if not rush to his rescue, which is what my instincts told me to do and is what I did. In spirit though not in fact I was older than Finnula Malloy and Red Eddie, who was younger still and thinner even than I and crippled as well, to take a maternal attitude toward the pair of them. So then and there and without a sound myself I swooped down on them and caught Red Eddie about the ankles and hauled them from beneath the table, Finnula riding, so to speak, on top of the boy she had been pinning there on the kitchen tiles. Then I took Finnula by one of her fleshy arms and pulled her up to her feet and at the same time tugged down her skirts and gave her a little shake.

And what has she been doing to you, Red Eddie?

She's been trying to kiss me. I won't have anyone trying to kiss me like that!

He was out of breath and pale, and his hair was wild, what with Finnula running her fingers through it and then her hands holding his poor crimped head as steady as her lust demanded. Red Eddie would not meet my eye and his mouth was as red and raw as if he had been foolishly licking his lips in a cold storm.

What have you to say for yourself, Finnula?

She had nothing to say, of course, and like her victim avoided my eye while nonetheless managing to flaunt her triumph as I had not yet seen any girl or woman do. She was a pretty sight, I must confess, with the heaving of her chest already womanly and the flush of her cheeks and even her arms and what I could see of her freckled chest, thanks to the dishevelment of the dress that was too small for her anyway and thus could not help but display the fullness of a shape that would never be mine. Have I said that Finnula had red hair? Such was the case and another cause for my envy and respect, which I took pains to hide, you may rest assured, as she stood there tossing back her lovely soft red hair and flaring her nostrils and smirking, totally self-preoccupied as if as soon as I turned my back she would have her way with Red Eddie, or in a sense already had. I do believe that she had no idea where she was or what I was saying.

You had better mind yourself, Finnula. If there is any more of this kind of thing there shall be consequences, you may be sure.

But if she came back to her senses then, or even if she did not, she knew she had nothing to fear from me, though as far as I know there was never a repetition of such young female awakening, or at least not under circumstances like those. For wasn't that the day of my own awakening? It was. And when darkness came at last and I lay in my narrow bed, smelling the formidable cleanliness of my bed linen, I could not help musing about Finnula, that plumpish girl brave in the pursuit of her sensations, which there in the darkness were mine as well, until sleep came to me and to Finnula herself, who lay not five beds from me and was almost recovered now from the flush and fervor of but a few hours before.

That night, then, I savored the darkness even more than usual, realizing that what Finnula had felt at the height of her bold selfhood was now rising in me as well, as I have said, no matter my sorry shape and unglamorous face and nondescript head of hair, and could not be stopped and would prove as powerful a tide as Finnula's. Once, before I slept, I chided myself for interfering with Finnula on the kitchen floor, then forgot the matter, knowing that Finnula's first kiss, if so it could be called, would be followed by a life of kissing. As would my own.

I have always best loved the night,

as I have said, have always favored it, though no girl at Saint Martha's was more energetic or committed to any day's activities than I. But just to add the final touch that will correct the initial impression I may have given of Saint Martha's, let me say that when one of us was afraid in the dark, as occasionally someone was, then the nightmares that brought a sudden sitting up of this one or that one of the girls ranged in their orderly rows of beds, were the nightmares that only an Irish foundling girl would ever tell, her thin voice trembling in the darkness as the dreamer huddled in the arms of an older girl or Foundling Mother herself. And of what were our girls afraid? Old women with long knots of hair. And hunchbacks. And bats. You could not have a proper

Irish nightmare without bats. Of course there were those nights of peaceful sleeping, and the night silence was undisturbed by so much as a sigh or whimper, when drowsily we would be brought awake by a woman softly singing at the end of the dark room where we were sleeping. Foundling Mother. Foundling Mother in her nightdress and arms crossed on her breast and singing.

I am not telling the life of Dervla O'Shannon, foundling. The life of a foundling is not so much. But love is another thing altogether. And I am speaking of love. My first love. My only love, no matter what anyone may say to the contrary.

Teddy. Teddy. Teddy my love.

Me Mum! Me Mum! Me! Me! Me!

Which is only the barest indication of the chorus of willingness and approval that met Foundling Mother's announcement and invitation that particular Sunday afternoon over the tea we most looked forward to throughout the week. And now it was getting on to the end of summer with a sweet mist gathered beyond the rusty grates and cookies and little cakes and bread and butter sandwiches heaped on the platters we could hardly raise to pass. We were already in the best of moods, laughing and nudging each other and trying to talk with our mouths full. Finnula Malloy, by then my truest friend as I might have known, was so full of herself and the warm and misty season that she was all but bursting out of her shape and skin, the lovely thing, tossing back her head of palest red hair and showing off her bosom, which vied with the immensity and brightness of her alarming eyes in gaining the covert attention of the room, though there was neither man nor boy present, until Foundling Mother stood up and tapped her cup with her spoon and we fell silent yet kept squirming the while, so to speak, for on such occasions Foundling Mother rarely failed to have something good to say to us, as this Sunday afternoon she did and better than that.

Well girls, you'll never imagine the wondrous thing that's come about. I could not believe the post when that letter came and asked myself why Major Minford should be writing to me of all people. Oh, you'll never believe the contents of that letter as I did not myself, though the main idea was modestly put, I must say, and was even phrased with uncertainty given Major Minford's stature and responsibility, of which not a soul in Carrickfergus is unaware, as I'm sure you know. A decorated soldier himself, girls, and director of the Old Soldiers' Home. Think of it! And what could such a man possibly be wanting of me or more importantly, of you? Just this. He wants to know if any of my foundling girls — you, he means — would like to volunteer to visit the Old Soldiers' Home periodically, say once a fortnight on a regular basis to liven up the lives of the old soldiers, perhaps with games and singing and dramatic skits — things like that as he suggests. What do you think of the idea, girls?

Which prompted a burst of cheering such as was rarely to be heard rising from our own playing field on a fine cold day when we were at the height of our prowess and glory too.

And who would like to volunteer for the kind of visits Major Minford envisions to the Old Soldiers' Home to brighten the hours of our national heroes?

Which prompted the shooting up of hands and the shouting and clamor and giving voice to our eager individual selves as I have already said. It was a burst of energy that one would not have expected the indolence of that late summer season to contain, and one that could not have gratified our Foundling Mother more, no matter that the smaller ones did not understand their own blissful agitation and did not know that when the time came they would be excluded from the volunteering they knew not what for, and that the oldest girls among us were somewhat more restrained than the rest in displaying what they thought of Major Minford's plan and their desire to participate in the surprises of the days to come because their added maturity, as we might say, tempered whatever enthusiasm they might have mustered for old men, heroes or not.

Ten years of age became the dividing line, which meant that those of us who had not yet attained that magical age, except for a determined few who were more developed than their number of years ordinarily allowed, were precluded even from the preparations necessary for our first visit to the Old Soldiers' Home and sullen or weeping were left in the care of Mrs. Jencks, who had her hands full, I can tell you, in trying to cheer up the raggle-taggle, as she called them, or put them to healthy occupation in the Foundling Home.

The rest of us set about our various new duties as officious and self-important as birds in a churchyard. The Foundling Mother herself arranged us in teams of three or four girls each and assigned us our tasks, one of which was procuring darts and boards and fell to the team consisting of myself and Finnula Malloy and little Moira Moylan, who by that time just slipped under the age barrier and had perhaps grown even worthier of whipping than when I had seen her that day in Foundling Mother's rooms. We were a good team of the kind of girl most trusted to get us a few games of darts.

The lesser teams, as my own group thought of them, ventured into Carrickfergus in high good humor not quite prepared to be denied, going from door to door with humility drawing the sweetness to their little faces as they stared up at him or her in the doorway and did their best to beg for books or games or anything that might set the old soldiers smiling up in Saint Clement's. Rarely did our girls return empty-handed, coming back to us as they did with at least a few items of sporting goods between them or piles of magazines tied up with string. And didn't we accrue quite a collection! I should say we did.

But Finnula Malloy and Moira Moylan and I had the best of it, since darts and dartboards might be found in private homes but were more likely to come to hand in pubs, which meant that we three girls had license in our own eyes at least to enter those drinking establishments for the male sex, as if the sanctioned nature of our quest bestowed on our persons a protective grace as invulnerable as the grace that was given us in church. Or so the matter appeared to me. But at the same time we could hardly know how we would be received or what disreputable situation might await us inside, which was surely what Finnula Malloy was hoping for since searching out the pubs was her idea in the first place, though her argument for pubs was purely based on reason. At least a wondrous uncertainty accompanied the pride with which we braved each pub we dared to enter, especially since minors were prohibited from such places, let alone women or young girls or girls who were hardly more than a breath or two from childhood, depending on the clear or cloudy eye that looked at us through the smoke of pipes or the smell of beer or strong drink. For if we were considered unassailably children then the sight of us would have been surprising but of no interest.

It would have been duller and more embarrassing for all concerned if we had been accompanied by Foundling Mother, which we were not, and which contributed to the excitement I am talking about to each and every occasion that we entered one of the pubs in question, from first to last of all the pubs of which Carrickfergus boasted. No doubt it was whispered that Foundling Mother was lax in letting us enter such places alone or even to enter them at all, but only those who did not believe in our mission could entertain such ungenerous thoughts. In point of fact Foundling Mother had not the slightest knowledge that any of her girls would stoop to using Major Minford's innocent plan as excuse, as it might have seemed to her, to go into such places where they were not allowed by law or otherwise. It was Finnula who promised us that Foundling Mother would never learn that we had invaded every pub in Carrickfergus and procured as many dartboards and accompanying darts as we could carry, all for bringing great joy to the old soldiers.

Canty's Pub was the first and of our trio I was the first to push my way inside and to hold open the door for the other two, no matter that Finnula was ordinarily the most brazen of the three of us, if I do say so. That day when first we stood together in Canty's Pub and the door closed behind us, even Finnula was trying to subdue her deep breathing and to prevent her face from showing what she

51

felt at the moment. The smoke was thick and the voices loud, our entrance even interrupted someone in the midst of a song. Oh, but the smoke cleared at once because of us, and the voices of the men, which we had never heard before in such a free and irreverent massing, ceased at the same time. Surely no crowded masculinity could save itself from immediate dissipation in the face of intruders such as ourselves, who were mere children on the one hand and shades of grown women on the other. It was as if unwanted sunlight had destroyed the beauty of a dark storm, and I felt quite ashamed for spoiling things for those men as we had done. In fact my self-consciousness or pure embarrassment for the self I thought they might see was nothing compared to the shame I felt for the men.

Canty himself came round from behind the bar, while the log that was hissing on the blackened hearth suddenly shifted its position as if our tremulous footsteps had disturbed the forces that held it in place, and then sighed and sent off a little shower of sparks that were dead before they settled on those hot stones. My eyes were already burning though the air was clear. Canty wiped his hands on his apron and smiled a smile that should have put us at our ease but did not.

And what have we here? To what do we owe the honor?

We are foundlings, Sir. From Saint Martha's up on the hill.

I see that by the way you're dressed. But how may I oblige you now?

Please Sir, we're collecting games

for the old soldiers up at Saint Clement's.

A worthy cause. A worthy cause indeed.

In particular, Sir, we're collecting games of darts.

Are you, then. But which do you mean, as loans or gifts?

We hadn't thought of that, Sir. Whatever you say.

Perhaps we needn't put such a fine point on the thing.

Mr. Canty was leaning down into the crescent we had formed, and giving us a kind regard, as I decided, looking from one to the other of us though it was I who did the talking, and letting his eyes settle just a moment longer on Finnula than on Moira and me, though Moira was second in gaining his attention, as I could tell, though I was oldest in attitude of the three. And why not? Why should he not have allowed himself a little more time to reflect on Finnula, since the way she had filled her incipient shape was enough to deserve the lingering of any man's attention, as I learned then with only mild regret. In fact, however, it was enough for me to have found my initial suspicions of him unworthy and to see how clean he was, from his white shirt to his white apron to the lively coloring of his skin, which indicated nothing so much as washing. He smelled of himself, I was happy to find, and not of beer or tobacco. It was a nice smell, as strong as the man himself was large, and was nothing less than the smell of cleanliness that you catch only on the breath and body of a man and not a woman, as I discovered then. Little Moira and even Finnula, despite her intuitive sense of the situation, were already unduly comfortable in Mr. Canty's presence, so I was glad when he raised himself up with a laugh and called out to someone I could not see just as we heard the hard sharp sound of a dart hitting home on a board.

Pat Hanley! Fire off your last, Pat! We want these young women to know that they shall always find a generous welcome in Canty's Pub!

How could we not? Even I was all but speechless when we had our board and our box of darts, and when Michael Canty himself, for such was his full name, patted us kindly on our shoulders and elsewhere too, according to Finnula, and opened the door and herded out the three of us. We

56

could not have been more encouraged and more emboldened and more elated as, each of us brooding on our first host in her own way, off we went to Foley's Pub and the Muckrose Inn and Laveren's and Reilly's, meeting with similar success on each of those visits in turn, though it was the first such visit we kept in our hearts and did not share in talking, as most young girls would.

That day, which was not the day of darts and pubs and the many days that succeeded that one, but was in fact the day we had been waiting for and had come at last, my bass drum resounded over Carrickfergus when, laden with our packages and prizes, except for myself since I bore my drum, we set off, marching down the hill through a warm clear steady rain. Because we chosen volunteers of Saint Martha's comprised the entire lot of us and hence were the only marchers there were that day, with no official parade of Carrickfergus called for that Sunday afternoon, naturally, and because our girls all carried gifts and bundles that would bring surprise and cheer to those for whom they were intended, I myself was the only instrumentalist performing in our parade that was not a parade, officially speaking. And the only reason I brought up the rear of our assemblage, striking my drum on every other beat, was to keep us all in step, though the sounding of my bass drum that day must have caused not a few citizens of Carrickfergus to think we were marching to the sound of doom or at least of some mournful event such as a funeral rather than to our first visit to Saint Clement's. Foundling Mother was in the lead and could not have been prouder of her girls, those of us who were such ready and clever volunteers, that is. Our faces were slick with rain and anticipation, our pace was lively despite the solemnity of my bass drum, which was as tall as I was and quite a load to carry, though I loved that drum and the identifying words painted in green on the drumheads, and could bear its hefty weight and beat on its sides the day long, I can tell you.

Infant girls in their mothers' arms or little girls who could scarcely manage to stay on their feet watched us from the windows and doorways of the stone cottages lining the upwardly climbing street toward the Old Soldiers' Home. The fewer cottages there were as the grade of the hill increased, the more female children there were in each, smiling and waving or scowling and sticking their thumbs in their mouths or beginning to cry as we went by, examples of the babes of Carrickfergus who were no better off than ourselves despite their christenings and their mummies and daddos all living together in the security, as at least the mummies and daddos falsely thought, of the family life of the Irish. As I have said or implied before, little did these poor souls know about the truth of things, despite the priests and records that appeared to certify them along the way.

All this while my drum boomed intermittently and Saint Clement's grew larger where it sat on the crest of that bare hill. Up we climbed, the sound of a few male voices beginning to reach us, so frail and high-pitched that they might have been the voices of little boys instead of men. But they were men, no matter their ages, as we soon found out for ourselves. We could see a couple of them clinging to the window grates, from within of course, and then hear them calling out in glee to their mates, and then see them disappearing from their posts at the open windows, still sentries of a sort after all these years.

Saint Clement's! Saint Clement's at last! And who could tell how many old soldiers were awaiting us and what they would think of us and we of them?

There was a great deal of pushing and shoving and chattering of our girls, as might be expected. And what with one thing and another, mainly the struggle I had to free myself of my cumbersome drum, all of them were well inside before I managed to make my way through the door and stand my drum against a bare wall and follow the voices of the girls and old men I could still not see. Oh, wasn't I hanging back a moment longer, doing my best to tidy my hair such as it was and look my best, which, along with my fiddling with the drum and finally leaning it against the wall, though not without a little concern for its safety, I can tell you, was just enough to cost me my place in line, so to speak, and leave me quite out of the party? I was. I was. For when I finally satisfied myself that I was ready and followed the siren sounds, as you may call them, of the foundling volunteers and the old men, and made what I thought might be a grand entrance, at least of sorts, what did I find but Finnula and Moira and Shivaughn and Molly and the rest of them happily ranged on rickety folding chairs about the cold immensity of that room that could not have been made hospitable, no matter how many paper banners had been strung by the steadier of the old gents in great celebrating loops from the top of each grated window to the next. They were not only seated around those perimeters and talking away in a fury, but each girl was already deeply engaged with this old soldier or that one already sitting beside Finnula or Moira or Molly or one of the rest of them, and leaving me out in the cold, so to speak, which was how I felt standing in the middle of that strangely empty room and alone. Alone! With not a single old soldier left for me! And a somewhat warped record playing a jaunty tune on the old Victrola and all those girls deep in the pleasures of entertaining those old men and waiting to see what would come of their efforts. But not me. Was it not just my wicked fate to be alone, standing there abandoned in the middle of that vast room and not even Foundling Mother to join me and help me bear such grievous humiliation? I had a good mind to turn around then and there and stalk unnoticed out of the place and march myself back alone to Saint Martha's and help Mrs. Jencks in keeping her raggle-taggle in line. I was that angry and forlorn and humiliated, as I have just said. And Divil take the drum, to use a well-known Irish word.

Which is what I would have done had I not felt from behind me a soft authoritative hand settling on my shoulder. It was the hand of a man unmistakably, if only for its size and firmness, though like a woman's too in its gentleness. That man was as good as his hand as I saw when I turned to him and looked up at him, forgetting in the moment the emptiness in which we stood, as on an island, with all around us the jabbering that might as well have been silence. He reminded me of someone, I don't mind saying, and there was no one he could have reminded me of, if not Michael Canty, which is exactly who he brought to mind though he was a different man altogether. At least on that point I was not deceived. Yet I could not look away from him, with his soft round shoulders and the bulk of his obviously large person, and his brownish eyes to match his soft black hair that was straight and fell nicely in a strand across one eye. If this was an old man, as I thought to myself, and as I believed he was despite his hair and the smoothness and ruddy comforting look of his face, then give me age, I thought, and spare me any youthful man as long as I live. He even had the pure Irish smell of Michael Canty, and it was a smell I both remembered and smelled anew, of a big man, an Irish man, that is, who might have just stepped from his bath. Then he spoke.

Minford. Major Minford. We can't allow you to be standing here alone like this!

I was thirteen years of age that moment and thus old enough to distrust such abrupt and discordant reversals of fortune. Old man indeed! Anyone could have seen he was not a day above sixty, if that, and anyone would have known that the best of old soldiers could not possibly have been saved for me. But it was a double dashing of hopes, to go from nothing to everything and be stupid enough to have been taken in on more than one count. Then to heap good fortune or misfortune, or vice versa or whatever you will, I quite loved Major Minford on the spot, a familiar situation that can as easily befall a grown woman as a young girl, which I would have known had Foundling Mother done her job.

What's your name, Love?

Dervla O'Shannon, Sir.

An uncommonly nice name, Dervla. Now come with me.

He was standing to my left side with his large right hand on my own right shoulder, so that we could not help but be close together, pressing together as a matter of fact, my slightness gathered firmly into the warmth and certainty of the man, and when he began to move and headed in the direction of one of the far corners, of course I could not help but move along at his side, and willingly, not even aware that my feet were moving thanks to the way he so slowly and pleasantly guided me against him, as if naturally wherever he went I would go too. All that time, which really amounted to no time at all, much to my sorrow, I was trying to twist myself to keep his pinkish placid face in view. He did not treat me like the poor young bad-tempered girl I was, he was that considerate, and took for granted that we should be crossing this emptiness together as we were.

Now Dervla, initially you must make a few allowances for Corporal Stack, who is by no means your typical old soldier. But if you'll trust me, Dervla, you'll find yourself well rewarded.

Oh, I thought, it was not a propitious beginning, abandoned as I was and as if I did not exist in the midst of the by now near riotous volunteers from Saint Martha's, and about to be fobbed off by Major Minford, whom I loved a bit less by now, onto some old corporal about whom even the major meant to warn me. But did Major Minford seriously believe in a happy outcome to my meeting with this old Corporal Stack, as he called him? And of what was he trying to warn me? Of course no warning, especially one so tactfully put, could have prepared me for the emotion with which I was then overcome. And the nature of this so unexpected emotion? Fright. A young girl's fright such as I had never known in all my years at Saint Martha's, bats and old women and hunchbacks notwithstanding. Fright it was and a fright that all but took me off my feet, I can tell you.

The source of it being that the little figure sitting alone in his dark corner and before whom we stood, trying to see him in the gloom and amidst the cobwebs, was dressed for battle no less. For battle! Which in itself should not have given me the fright it did, though the festive situation made his preposterous getup surprising enough and inappropriate to say the least. Many of the old soldiers gathered together to receive the volunteers from Saint Martha's were dressed on that occasion in military regalia or portions thereof from another day, so that Corporal Stack's costume was not in itself enough to cause me the shock and fright it did. Even the helmet of a quarter century or so in the past might have been surprising but not in itself, again, enough to nearly set me off my feet as I have said. But in combination with the mask strapped about his head and concealing his face, then helmet and mask together were quite sufficient to shock the unsuspecting girl I was and to give me the fright of my life.

Yes, a mask. A gas mask. A contraption of stiffened cloth and dangling straps and great gogglelike eyes and a length of black rubber hose protruding from where the nose should have been. Initially I did not identify the incongruous mask in which Corporal Stack was concealing his face, but found myself staring down at some monstrous improbability of an old soldier with the face of a menacing bug, mainly because of the immense and sightless eyes and the mechanical snout. When I was suddenly able to put a name to the outlandish face and recognize it for what it was, a vintage gas mask of the time of the trenches, of which I had specific knowledge because Mrs. Jennings's brother had been a victim of a gas attack in the

Great War, failing to extract his mask from its canvas pouch in time to save his lungs from severe damage, still the initial fright stayed on. For no matter the sense I was able to make of Corporal Stack's tin helmet as that kind was called, and the mask intended to protect him from waves of mustard gas rolling across muddy seas of the dead, the look of him could not have been more unsettling for a young girl like me. Even when I had satisfied myself that he was human after all and not some creature devised by a fiend, I could not rid myself of the feeling that at the least he looked like a waxen mannequin modeling the battle dress of the First World War. There might have been moths concealed in the pockets and creases of that old uniform, as it seemed to me.

Thus I had my introduction to Corporal Stack, which was the worse for me as I thought, though I noted that Major Minford showed no signs of discomfort on his pinkish face and was in fact smiling down at the little disfigured old soldier in his corner with a most benevolent and becoming comradeship. At least Major Minford's hand on my shoulder was a lovely massive reminder of the rest of him, despite the fact that as I say my ardor was cooling. In the meanwhile a few of our girls had persuaded their old partners to join them dancing, and the darts that Finnula and Moira and I had contributed to the party were beginning to fly.

You may come out now, Corporal. There's a young lady to see ya.

Certainly, this poor old soldier

named Stack was not hard of hearing, whatever else his impairments might have been. For no sooner had the kindly major leaned down to him and spoken in those kindly tones that said there was nothing so very out of the ordinary with the immovable corporal after all, then quick as little Moira whisking away an extra slice of holiday cake for herself, off came the helmet, as if the old soldier was only too willing to have an excuse to rid himself of the weight on his head, which was then followed by the mask as well.

How's that, Major? A young lady?

As if he could not see me clearly enough where the major was hugging me to his side and I was already divesting myself of my shock and fear. Another dart went by like a wasp to its victim and I heard Finnula's laugh through the noise.

Just so, Corporal. But mind you, we must have no more sham senility to-day!

Very good, Sir.

Whereupon Major Minford released my shoulder and said he would be leaving the two of us together then, and looking as if he had done even more than what had been wanted of him on my behalf, turned and took himself off like some gracious officer taking leave of his lady at a fancy military ball. Let him go, I told myself but with a momentary pang nonetheless, especially when I saw him heading in the direction of Mrs. Jennings.

Just my ugly old-fellow's luck! A room full of the pick of Ireland's girls, with a single exception, and look who I draw but the exception!

I knew my place well enough to make no reply to that remark. I thought of all we girls had done and all I had personally accomplished to be where I was and wished that the Old Soldiers' Home was not so similar to Saint Martha's except for a certain dust and gloom about the place which may have been understandable given that its inhabitants were progressing toward their certain end, enfeebled every last one of them, heroes or not, whereas Saint Martha's was home to a crowd of thriving girls with all the world ahead of them, unwanted as we may have been or not.

No doubt he made his usual uncomplimentary comments?

Beg pardon, Sir?

Minford. Whispering derogatory things behind my back?

Oh no, Sir. He did nothing of the sort. Quite the opposite.

Which happened to appease him as I had hoped it would. He stared up at me still frowning and narrowing his eyes, doubting my truthfulness against his will, and then and with a suddenly different expression on his face, no doubt having forgotten the ruse of his initial suspicion, looked me up and down slowly, appraisingly, which made me uncomfortable and yet proud at the same time.

Sit down, why don't ya. I'm not in the mood for dancing.

I'm not much for dancing myself, Sir.

You may stop the Sir-business if you don't mind.

But should I then just call you Corporal Stack?

No you should not. As of this moment forward I am Teddy to you.

At this point I thought he would demand to know my own name or at least hint that he would be pleased to know it, and I confess I was disappointed when he did not, especially since I liked the sound of Teddy and was convinced that he would be happily surprised when he finally heard the full resonance of Dervla, a very attractive name clothed in a certain innuendo as I intuited even when I was no more than a young girl awaiting her growth.

I invited you to sit down. So you must do as I say.

Awkwardly and remembering myself I obeyed him without a word, for I could not so easily dispense with the more formal language that acknowledged the respect for my elders that of course I had been taught along with all the rest by Foundling Mother. I knew that it would be time yet before I could say aloud his name let alone naturally and without extreme discomfort, though truth be known I was allowed to be my own self with Teddy a good deal sooner than I had thought.

Now everyone. Your attention, please . . .

It was Foundling Mother, wouldn't you know, standing in the middle of the room and interrupting us as if it took only my thought of her to bring her suddenly to life, causing the phonograph to slow to a stop in midtune and the darts to die in the hand before they could be thrown.

Now everyone, if you will just stop your dancing and put aside your games and step outside, you shall see before you a spectacle — perhaps activity is the proper word — that cannot help but soar above the glories of this special day!

And clapped her hands as if to urge us on while Teddy leaned over and raised a shielding hand and grumbled into my ear — Children. Tiny children. With some kind of infantile skit to perform. As if we were all children, and just when you and I were getting acquainted. I told you Minford was not to be trusted.

Truth to tell, I shared Teddy's resentment and wished that Foundling Mother had left us to our own devices, no matter what she and the major had cooked up.

Come along, Dervla!

And you too, Corporal Stack . . .

The two of them standing there together and feigning smiles and clapping hands like the keepers of gabbling geese and sheep and calling out specifically to Teddy and me, for suddenly he and I were the only ones still left in the room, that much already absorbed in each other but having no way out and nothing to do except comply.

Ah damn the two of 'em. Where's my cane?

Let me reach it for you, Teddy.

Which I did, of course, since it was an imposing cane of heavy smooth black wood rounded at one end in perfect symmetry for the hand and bearing at its other end a giant rubber tip to prevent slipping on whatever smooth surface its invalided carrier might encounter. So the ugly thing, of the sort you might find in hospitals rather than the kind of gloriously gnarled stick you might see a gentleman out walking with, was lying beside Teddy's chair and clearly visible.

Have you difficulty in getting about, Teddy?

Just for show. A sign of my exalted station.

I had nothing to say to that, of course, though I was unaccountably relieved.

Everyone was crowded round together in the middle of the old soldiers' playing field and there was a fair breeze lifting the hair and hearts of everyone so gathered. The field was much like our own field except that it was intended for drilling and marching and so forth as well as football, and further was never used, as was evident by its covering of tall unruly grass smelling of sweetness itself on that spring breeze. Slowly, arm in arm, as if I might support one side of him while the ugly cane took care of the other, Teddy and I approached that crowd of bareheaded girls and old men who, impressed by Teddy's stately progress or knowing him for the sham he was, suddenly opened their circle to make way for us and to reveal the surprise that Foundling Mother had promised us and that but a moment before had been concealed behind the sheltering bodies of girls and heroes. A great clapping arose on the fair breeze.

Horses!

That was me exclaiming and with genuine delight, I can tell you.

Ponies. They are only ponies. Has

that woman taught you nothing, Dervla?

I was much taken aback to hear Teddy saying my name as naturally as if we were intimates. In fact I was so busy savoring the sound of it on Teddy's voice, which was reassuringly deep for the small size of him, that I was only able to mumble something to the effect that Foundling Mother was a very good teacher no matter what he might think of her, but that truth be known I was quite unfamiliar with horses or ponies either, though I soon came to know that the horse was Ireland's gift to the world, along with women and drink and the singing of verses. For the time being I remained in my declared ignorance of the mighty horse, real or legendary.

The animals before us, of which

there were three, looked like overly large stuffed toys that had been splattered with mud and then left to dry, they were that filthy. They must have been extremely old as well for they merely drooped their heads and stood as if they would never move again, despite the girls throwing their arms about their necks and patting them all over from nose to tail. The eyes in the poor creatures' heads were half hidden by drooping lids, though insofar as one could see them, the eyes of those ponies were sick and sad with rheum.

Pony rides! They mean to give us pony rides! The nerve of 'em!

Of course I could not share Teddy's indignation since no matter the wretched condition of those immense old ponies, I might have been a mere five-year-old girl, I was that enthralled by the sight of them, with the warm breeze stirring their miserable tails and their coats of long hair except where matted down by the mud. But Teddy was right. The ponies were for the entertainment of the old soldiers, and I did understand Teddy's point of view and the inappropriateness of the idea, which was Foundling Mother's own as Major Minford announced with a grateful flush on his long thick Irish face. In the course of that speech, which he offered the entire assembly before anyone could ride, he also thanked Mr. Lackey of Lackey's Livery Stable for providing these grand ponies which that generous person had gone to great trouble to bring up to us in a van. Mr. Lackey was plainly older than any old soldier in the group, but also, with his little bowed legs and shorter even than my Teddy, was as spry as any man of any age could possibly be, grinning away and sparkling his eyes and wearing his crumpled felt hat cocked at a jaunty angle atop his head. He wore soiled riding britches and carried a length of rattan stick with which to enforce obedience from his animals. He smelled more strongly of horses and stables than did his ponies, as I discovered when circumstances found me briefly and before I could extricate myself, within smelling distance of Mr. Lackey.

Round and round they began to go, Mr. Lackey and the major and Foundling Mother each at the head of one of the ponies and each pony bearing an old soldier flanked on either side by foundling girls to hold him on while the rest of those aged men stood by waiting their turns. It was great fun except for the girls, who had nothing to do but watch until they should be called upon to assist in the operation and hence had time to reflect that they wished that they themselves were riding. The moving ring of old men and near-dead ponies looked like a charmed circle thanks to the rather silly happiness of the old riders, who had known nothing out of the ordinary since they'd been blown from the trenches so long ago and survived to end up at the Old Soldiers' Home. At least they had not a shred of that pride with which Teddy was cursed, as it seemed to me, since he had refused a turn on one of the ponies and clearly considered himself too good to participate in any way in what was going on. Except at the end, when each and every old soldier had had his riding to his heart's content, though he was only led about like a child, suddenly Major Minford turned to Teddy, who was standing somewhat apart with me, and singled him out and in the next moment of ensuing silence with all eyes upon us, and showing Teddy his warmest Irish smile, which indicated that he was not a major for nothing and was not to be disobeyed, insisted that Teddy take his turn after all, if only to show proper gratitude to Mr. Lackey and to complete the flowering of that day.

Very well, Sir. But I shall not be led.

As you will, Corporal Stack. But I want no accidents today.

You may trust me, Sir.

So Teddy handed me his cane and borrowed Mr. Lackey's rattan stick and requested a little help so as to climb upon the back of the old pony of his choice, and then asking Foundling Mother to let go if she would and step away, for it was the pony she had been leading that Teddy had selected for his ride, off he went as briskly as you please and looking as if he might disappear off the edge of the field, so confidently did he hold the reins and wield Mr. Lackey's stick. As for the pony, the poor thing recovered its youth at the first blow and picked up its feet and perked up generally, knowing beyond a doubt that the rider on his back meant business. It was a grand sight, as he who had appeared unable to walk except with a cane and great difficulty, sat lightly on that pony and with his legs pressed the creature this way and that with little need of the stick once they got going. From being nearly out of sight they returned to us at a nice canter, as Teddy later told me it was called, and then circled beautifully to the right and then to the left and all at once came to a smart halt directly in front of us and Teddy hopped off and handed Mr. Lackey his stick. The pony stayed exactly where Teddy left him, too afraid of his missing rider to move so much as a step from where that missing rider meant him to be. And as Teddy nonchalantly walked back to me, everybody clapped and cheered and I basked in Teddy's glory.

That night there was no sleeping in our dormitory filled with the light of the stars and darkness at the end of that late summer's day and the whispering of irrepressible girls telling what had happened to them and how they had frolicked with their partners. Through the all but silent ring of their sweet voices I heard my own closest friend, Finnula Malloy, whispering loudly to Moira Moylan about how she had sat upon the lap of her jolly old rifleman, as she called him, to which Moira replied that that was nothing and she could tell better if she dared, which I gathered she did by the less than audible but more confidential sound of her. On it went, with little piping questions interrupting the stories, and laughter suddenly obscuring it all. Not once did Foundling Mother appear to tell us it was time to be quiet, preoccupied I suppose with her own private musings on the major.

As for me, I said not a word that night and paid little attention to the whispering. I was awake but too content to behave like a child or young girl. My contentment was too serious to share.

Dear Foundling Mother,

Here I am, as you can see, safe and welcomed, truly, into Corporal Stack's munificent family — or what is left of it, that is. And do you know, dearest mother of our own Saint

Martha's, that I cannot say what enthralls me more, your trust in me and sanctioning of my visit to the Stack family, or the different perspective that the Stack family has given me on the nature of nurturing which seems to make the bells ring in the village church, though there is not a soul inside to ring them.

I miss you.

Never in my life did it occur to me that I might live and breathe out of the sound of your voice and sight. But such is the case, as I now know. Also, Foundling Mother, never have I had the slightest awareness that there might be another way to live than the way we do at Saint Martha's. But so there is.

I miss you.

Could I fail to understand that indeed I must have taxed your good judgment that day I carried Corporal Stack's invitation into your presence to hear me out and, after a question or two and on your dear face a thoughtful look I had never seen before, and after the several days it took you to confer with Major Minford, to give me to know that, yes, I had your permission to visit High Crosses of Kells, when in fact I was not even sure I wanted to? I understood the gravity of the thing since no young girl's purity, my own included, is to be counted on for sure.

Breathe easy, Foundling Mother. I miss you. I am worthy of the faith you have placed in me.

I have been here at High Crosses of Kells three nights or perhaps only two, and with the greatest possible confidence am pleased to state that there has been no incident or person of a tempting sort, which is to say that I am as good a girl as I was when you extracted my little self from the basket.

Trust me, then.

I shall write you daily or try to, and in my next shall give you the things and people I have omitted here for the sake of my main purpose, which has been to express my thanks on my knees as I might say, along with my reassurance.

Please preserve my letters that I might read them all together on my return.

This letter, as I now admit, was true in sentiment but in every other way as false as a cat. Teddy laughed when he read it, slapping his leg with his cane and prompting in me a faint sweat of humiliation.

Dervla, my dear, you're a liar! Nothing more than an out-and-out liar and I fail to see how you could possibly write such a thing as this and to such a woman as your presumptive mother when anyone with a glimmer of sense must know that what she's preparing for herself and my major is a fine example of that woman's fitness for the stews, as aren't they all.

But Teddy, it was you yourself told me to write this letter and what to say!

There you go, tryin' to shovel the whole thing onto me! By no means did I advise you to go into this business about trust and virtue as if you were an orator for sure and trained since a babe in the deceptions of the Latin language, and not just a poor young girl who's won my heart.

Which we may lay at your door as well, Teddy.

Oh no you don't! Tryin' to put another unseemly accusation on my back when it was you who started it and has lured me on for sure. But I'll tell you this, Dervla my girl, I'll not lay a hand on you until you reach sixteen years of age, and no equivocating either.

So I must wait then, Teddy?

That you must. And I'll tell you another thing my precious girl. I'll not have Lackey making advances. I'll not have it! If the little bugger puts so much as a finger on you, Dervla, he'll answer to Corporal Stack, and that, my child, is something you wouldn't want to see.

But it was all Mr. Lackey's doing, and there's the truth of it. Had it not been for Mr. Lackey and my aversion to the smell of him, I suppose that Teddy and I might have been content to share our fortnightly meetings and sit in our corner holding hands but refusing all the entertainment except when it came to the ponies, the wretched things. Perhaps without Mr. Lackey's smell I might have thought of nothing other than Teddy and been satisfied with little more than mere thoughts and dreams while Teddy himself sat up there at Saint Clement's waiting for nothing more than the sound of my drum. But Mr. Lackey was always there with his ponies and eagerness to please, that little bow-legged man inseparable from his pathetic unkempt animals and smelling more of his stables than did his ponies themselves. Oh, how he smelled of manure and darkness, and how I disliked the way he smelled! Which surely in the back of his mind he knew, for the more I tried to avoid him or give myself a little breathing space in his presence, the closer he came, smiling, as if I could not possibly have found his eager little person anything other than how he thought of himself, let alone repellent. So just let Teddy be taking his fortnightly ride on Ducky, for so the poor creature was named, than Mr. Lackey crowded in on me with all the gaping and cheering onlookers giving him good cover, so to speak, and even then in all pretended innocence and good fellowship, as he would have had me think, feeling me here and there with his little callused irrepressible hands, which would have struck my Teddy dumb, had he only known. Of course it takes two to make a custard as Foundling Mother used to say, mystifying the general lot of us until with aging we began to understand. And I suppose that being the tall, skinny, irritable girl that I was, I must have thrown off a smell of my own distinctive kind despite myself, and which Mr. Lackey could not resist. Then there was Teddy whispering into my receptive ear that skinny girls are quicker to return a kiss and the rest of it than are your hefty good-humored girls, public-house opinion notwithstanding.

The point being that Mr. Lackey

soon enough revealed his plan. Which was? Only that Teddy and I should come to live in Lackey's Livery Stable, where Teddy would enjoy a daily ride on Ducky and I should learn the rudiments of horsemanship on Cooky, as the other poor little beast was called, and accompany Teddy for long happy jaunts into the forbidden realm of the country round. All of us understood that Mr. Lackey did not mean forever and that the ponies and riding and all that was offered up as an enticement, though all three of us also understood to varying degrees that Mr. Lackey had more than riding in mind, which is why Teddy held his tongue just long enough to devise a way that the preposterous scheme might come to pass, which was by deception. For suddenly he longed to

be free of Saint Clement's and assumed that I felt the same about Saint
Martha's, as I both did and didn't,
trying to imagine days and nights
without the foundlings I had always
known and Foundling Mother herself.
The idea was nothing less than, as I
have already said, that Teddy and I
must live on Mr. Lackey's premises,
and for this my Teddy's Major Minford and my own Mrs. Jennings would
never in all their days, as Teddy said,
give their approval or permission
either. But if Teddy proposed a visit
to his family at High Crosses of Kells?
And suggested that I travel along with
him to hold his cane when necessary
and to have the enjoyment of staying
a while on the Stack farm near the
town with such a pretty name? Why
then the major and Foundling Mother

might acquiesce and send us off with their blessings. One mouth less to feed in either institution, as Teddy thought they might envision it.

Thus and so as Teddy said when he began to shovel out the knee-deep stalls of Lackey's Livery Stables and I wrote my letters and Mr. Lackey fondled me in the darkness as I allowed so that I should not attain the age of womanhood entirely unprepared for Teddy.

Dearest Foundling Mother,

As of this cold and rainy hour, I find myself missing more than ever my empty bed in Saint Martha's, and more than ever missing you yourself, dear Foundling Mother. It is one thing for a child, which I still consider myself to be, maturing factors aside, to find herself thrilling to the adventure of a new life, and quite another to grieve as I am grieving for the home she has forfeited, no matter how temporarily, as the price she has had to pay for her pleasure.

As I wrote so long ago as it seems to me and must to you as well, the very fact that the Stack family is situated on a farm, so unfamiliar as it must be to a girl who, like the rest of the girls of Saint Martha's in Carrickfergus, has never as much as taken a walk in the country, excited my attention as much as Mrs. Stack's first welcome relaxed my worries and from the start provided the security any child needs. The farm is run-down, I fear, and Mrs. Stack, who is nothing more than a distant cousin of Corporal Stack, is in fact a woman too lofty, in my opinion, in her handling of the poor Stack foundlings, of which there are a goodly number and all of them lacking any comprehension whatsoever as to why they are here in the first place.

On the Stack farm, then, there are children, most of them entirely new to Corporal Stack, who crowd the hearth or sit in dark corners giving vent to their miseries while Mrs. Stack stands lecturing to this little thing or another who cannot stay upright on her two feet for the count of three let alone comprehend the lecturing of Mrs. Stack who thinks that Irish morality, which is a strange concept you will agree, is essential to the foundling even before the poor thing can begin to keen. The work I do as houseguest of Corporal Stack's distant cousin is considerable.

But the farm, Foundling Mother, the farm! There is a goat for milking, and a cow who has gone permanently dry, and an old horse who is free to follow about after Mrs. Stack's old father who walks but a short distance from the house to empty what he calls his cursed bladder bag, the old horse stopping every time and joining the old man in this frequent ritual, as if the ancient animal suffered the exact same inner failing as the man. Teddy tries to keep me from seeing, but I am a quick girl, as you if anyone must know, and there is not much I don't see. And mud, dear Foundling Mother, and manure, which must to you sound quite unattractive but to me are the first surprises of the natural world into which I sink to my knees no less and with exactly the same abandon as one of Mrs. Stack's youngest. Imagine, a girl as mature as myself acting like a tiny child just because she has never before stepped into a sea of mud or onto an old barn's flooring of manure! Oh, but this worldly muck is harmless, no matter how it reeks of decomposition.

I miss you.

The wind is howling, Mrs. Stack is reading aloud from a lofty book too heavy to hold, while the babies are laughing senselessly or weeping for they know not what . . .

Run-down? Mud and manure?

What's got into that head of yours to picture my own Stack family so low! If you're going to make them up, Dervla, couldn't you give me a few grand relations and a farm to be proud of? All smiles and plenty and none of these babies crawling about in such consternation? As for that old gent and the ancient horse pissing in unison, I cannot for the life of me see how even you could have come up with that bit or how you expect your Mrs. Jennings to believe such stuff, which as you and I both know is the point. Oh, you've a wicked imagination, Dervla. Wicked!

I hung my head, the fumes of the ponies rose around us in the darkness. Mr. Lackey was hovering about somewhere just waiting to have a go at me. I defended my letter.

Please, Teddy, I don't know anything about grand people. Besides,
you don't think Mrs. Jennings reads
my letters, do you? Besides, people
will believe anything at all if it's writ-
ten down. Besides, I'm only writing
about myself, Teddy, I'm that un-
happy if you only knew.

Oh, now Dervla, we'll just tack up
these ponies and go for a nice ride!

Dearest dearest
Foundling Mother,

I am happy to be at High
Crosses of Kells, which I say for
fear I might have given you a false
impression. Mrs. Stack's grandness of mind and manner is winning me over, no matter that none
of her babies with their stunned
expressions and weepy eyes has

the wit to understand a word she says.

Is my bed still empty? Oh, I know it is, for despite the desperate need with which you must forever contend, and I know you would never turn away a foundling as long as you, dear Foundling Mother, are directress of Saint Martha's, I know you will save me my empty bed just as it was when I departed. I know you will.

My labors are many as I have mentioned. Yet they are different from my tasks at Saint Martha's and I enjoy them all. Who would not work readily for such a lady as Corporal Stack's distant cousin, who as a young girl read entire libraries and hence developed her lofty ways with even the most helpless child, which I now admire. Between my many chores I listen to Mrs. Stack reading aloud in her fine voice about the Prince of Deveren or help her to make sausages or slaughter geese for the table. The Prince of Deveren, incidentally, slays a terrible creature called Paky and for his shining goodness is canonized by a great bishop in the local church, which, says Mrs. Stack, is how our Irish morality was born.

Hold me, Foundling Mother! Hold me!

I shall be returning soon.

You shall not! And is it not painfully clear that you're going from bad to worse as the fellow says? Why should you be thinking of Irish morality and the rest of it? You're not only a liar, Dervla, but something even I cannot put a name to.

Forgive me, Teddy.

The country round, as I soon discovered, was never the same from one moment to the next, and was dark and rolling and frightening even if the sun shone and there were no evil caravans in sight, which there usually were. Out we rode, Teddy and I, side by side on our ponies as filthy as ever, for even with my determination I could not make them yield up their coats of mud and matted hair, and within a few reluctant steps of our sad ponies the road left Lackey's Livery Stable far behind and took us through an alley of wet trees and another and another and then, with a sudden breath, into the country which, as we all know, had been denied me all my life and for good reason, as on those first days of riding out I understood full well.

It was a mean and frightening sight from empty road to distant horizon everywhere we looked, and never the same but closed in there by black slopes of barrenness and there by a stand of distant trees inside a circlet of the cruelest briars. Miles away from where we rode a miserable stone bridge lifted its broken back over a swollen stream, and fields and woods and distances and roads were all the same, every one of them, so empty

115

that there must be unfriendly figures lurking where we could not see them but knew they were. Sometimes there was the sound of hounds with their jaws open, sometimes a black rain that passed us by or trapped us unaware in its downpour. There were hills and crags far off and empty cottages closer by. Even the rainbows that suddenly appeared were small and devastated and so pale of color as to be nothing less than portentous, as if only harm could lie in wait for us in those distant fields where the rainbows rose and fell with joy to no one, even to Teddy and me. Distant animals disappeared as we drew close, occasionally smoke rose from sorry farmhouses we never saw, or not for long. Nothing was pre-dictable out there. Any sort of man at all might appear before us on the road we followed or some other, for it was a vast world laced with empty roads, or come out at us from the bracken to either side of us as we listened to the thunder and the cries of a ewe. No wonder the country round was forbidden to the girls of Saint Martha's. No wonder we were not allowed to venture forth upon it. Without Teddy, I was convinced, I would never find my way back to Lackey's Livery Stable since even the proverbial instincts of horse and pony were no match for those ever-changing shapes or narrow roads without signs or markers, and surely I could not depend on the likes of Cooky, lowest of the low when it came to ponies, to find her way back to hay and steaming buckets of feed should I ever lose Teddy and be left alone out there.

I thought of such things when I rode out with Teddy. But wasn't I the girl to give myself to dangers? I was! And riding beside him I did not truly think that harm could come to us, though I knew it might, and that was the pleasure of the day and my mistake.

It came to us in the form of a sound and from behind our backs, sinister surprise as it turned out to be, and at the moment we first heard it, and simultaneously, though neither Teddy nor I was willing to call the other's attention to the slowly approaching roar or whatever it was, Ducky and Cooky stopped dead in their tracks, dumb as they were, admitting forcefully enough what Teddy and I could not. There were no obstructions to either side of us and this day the country fell away far and wide in all its blackness and clouds with sunlight coming down coldly here and there and nothing to see. Closer came the fearsome sound. Closer came what might have been the sound, intimidating for sure, of falling rocks somewhere or suddenly rushing water or perhaps the thunder of beating wings, and all this from behind us and so filled with purpose that even our all but insensate ponies began to tremble. Poor Ducky and Cooky, hanging their heads and, no matter how much I disliked the two of them, shivering in fright and refusing to take so much as a single step forward on that country road. Louder it grew, that sound I decided was more like the thundering of wings, and only at the last moment did I manage to look over my shoulder and see what was bearing down on us and quickly too.

Teddy! Watch out, Teddy!

For what did I see in that single wide-eyed glance? Horses, as one might have thought, and dogs, and men and women astride those galloping horses and swarming in the road behind us with their pink coats and faces as shrill as the horn the fattest of the old fellows blew. It seemed to me an army though it was only some unruly hunt that was surely now at the end of its chase though Teddy and I had seen no animal of any sort, fox or stag or whatever it was they were after. For those horses were ready to drop, so far had they come and so fast and heavy were they galloping down upon us, and the shrill dogs were hanging out their tongues for the kill. And there we stood, Teddy and I and Ducky and Cooky, stock-still and directly in the path of those barbarians in their fancy clothes!

Jump, Teddy! Jump!

Yet poor fool of a man that he was, or poor fool of a man in motionless pursuit of his destiny, for that he was, he did no such thing but simply sat on Ducky as straight upright as he could, too stern to get out of the way, too proud to sacrifice his dignity to a hundred unruly foxhunters with their dogs and horses and bright faces and flying whips.

There was a woman, oddly enough as I thought at the time, and a very young woman she was too, coursing at the head of that savage pack, and though I looked up at her from where I lay in the frozen ditch and though our eyes met, her pale young face betrayed not a flicker of concern for me, or more importantly, for Teddy, at whom she looked with the deadliest possible indifference and then looked away, beyond him, into the country round where their quarry ran. I watched, I cried out, and up went the young woman on her lathered horse and before my eyes jumped over Teddy and Ducky too as if the pair of them were nothing more than a stone wall or an Irish bank. Jumping over Teddy, and her young face as white and sharp as the blade of an ax and her great horse gathering itself and leaping up and over as it had been doing all the day, except that that girl's beast must have been tired or careless for even as I lay in the ice and brambles I saw a rear hoof clip my Teddy in the back of his head, while the dogs breathed furiously upon me, running on, and the rest of the hunt swerved to either side of my fallen Teddy like a black tide parting around a rock.

They were gone. The silence denied that they had ever swept over us and passed our way, except for the turmoil in the mud, and the hoofprints, and the brambles trampled upon and torn. And except for Teddy, stretched out flat as he was.

It began to rain.

To think! The nerve! Why, who could believe that that young woman had jumped my Teddy without a qualm as it seemed to me, that she jumped over a man on a pony without even trying to pass him to either side. And then not to jump him clear but to allow one of her horse's hooves as

big as a queen's crown to catch my
Teddy in the back of the head and not
only to knock him from Ducky's back
clean as a whistle, which was one of
Teddy's favorite expressions, but to
leave him as for dead on the road, as
he might have been when I crawled
across to him and whispered his
name.

Teddy! Speak to me, Teddy!

But he did not, no matter my fright-
ened breath on his face or the sound
of my young voice as I begged him to
come round and back to me. There
we lay, the two of us, without our
ponies that had disappeared, the little
divils, and emptiness pressing upon us
from far and near. Then I heard another sound. I propped myself on my
elbows and breathed my warm breath
down upon Teddy's lifeless look of

him, and again could not believe what I was hearing. The sound of a great motorcar for sure, and bearing directly down upon us from this direction or that one, for we were lying where two meandering dirt roads crossed. Then it was upon us, an enormous chocolate-colored automobile sweating there in the rain, and hardly had it come to a halt than the very girl who had jumped over my Teddy, and with the selfsame lack of consideration, stepped from that auto, in no hurry either, and still dressed for riding horses bid me help her carry Teddy to the car.

Is he dead, Miss? Tell me he's not dead! . . .

Oh get up, you, and give me a hand.

It was a girl's voice, make no mistake, yet as flat and rude as might have been the voice of an old gent talking down to an illiterate boy. She was about my height and as thin as myself, differing from me only in coloring, with her blonde hair that belonged in a book never intended for the likes of me, and in her mud-bespattered fox-hunting getup which she still wore, and in something about her that finally came to me as her age. Yes, her age. For it was her age that I feared as much as anything else that first day when she who had victimized my Teddy came to his rescue. What a lithe still-sweating thing she was and straight from the castle with only the cruelest disdain for the foundling I was, though who or what I was mattered not at all to that person as I full well knew at the time, even in my distraction for Teddy.

Take his feet, will you. I'll take the head.

Which told the whole story, though never would I have let my own feelings stand in the way of Teddy's saving, and told myself that day that it should not be for long and that this girl, called Heather, as I later learned, to my Thistle, we were that close in most respects, except for the castle and farmyard and of course her age, would merely bring my Teddy round in a flash and in a flash return us to Mr. Lackey, smell and all, as I would indeed have welcomed the sight of him. But it was not to be.

Together we two skinny girls, that similar for all our miles apart, struggled with my poor inert Teddy, all dangling now in arm and leg and of a weight I never could have expected, until we finally got him stretched out nicely on the backseat with the officious girl's pink coat rolled up for a pillow. I knelt on the back floor of the family car, as it turned out to be, and held one of Teddy's hands in mine while Heather, who soon enough told me I must call her Miss and nothing so familiar as the name she was known by, sat behind the rocking round wooden steering wheel like a child, and drove us off, taking all the care she could for the jouncing thanks to the ruts in the road, I'll give her that. Nonetheless we suffered a fair amount of bouncing about and the smell inside that otherwise majestic car was toxic, for beyond the richness of the leather there came the deadly vapors of the petrol. From where I crouched in the back of the grand old car with

Teddy, who had still not stirred eye or limb and was not breathing so as to make me easy, now and then I glanced up and around to catch a glimpse of the blonde hair and the narrow shoulders. Even in my apprehension about Teddy, something I could not place about that blonde girl kept nagging at me and exciting more than my envy. Fear it was. An arousing of my jealous nature. But of what had I to be jealous, hair and castle and ability to operate a vehicle I had never even seen in my life aside? Jealous of what that was the source of my fear as well? She was a person of few words as Teddy used to say, but she let me know from the heights of her superiority before the ride's end.

Sixteen she was.

Not that!

Yes, she was. Sixteen! So now on top of everything else I must worry about her age that I was still so short of attaining. Oh, and Teddy would recognize her age and its significance in one sly flutter if he just lived and ever again opened his eyes. His romantic eyes. No wonder I was so cast down and apprehensive when we arrived at Great Manor, which was not a castle but as good as one, and as big as Saint Martha's or Saint Clement's and no institutional dwelling either but more spacious, you might say, and more comfortable. Indeed you could put all the old soldiers of Saint Clement's inside that brooding place and still have room enough for Foundling Mother's girls, whereas there were a mere three souls living in that house, discounting a couple of old servants and the dogs. Never had I had to fight so hard for my pride in myself as I did that day, and nearly lost it, too.

George! William! Carry that man to the house. And you, you can just come with me.

But Miss . . . I'm sworn to Teddy! I cannot leave him now in his worst!

To which she did not deign to reply but set off briskly with her leather boots tight on her slender calves and her heels imperious on the cobble-stones and her bare arms swinging as if she cared nothing at all for the fine coat we had left on the seat of the car. I hurried to follow, you may be sure, leaving the car with three doors open in the stableyard where we had stopped, just as a young boy led from the barn the very beast, rugged up and larger than ever, who had dealt my Teddy such a ferocious blow. Round they went, boy and horse, the animal three times the height of the boy and walking with a sad loping stride and hanging head as if the poor beast knew well enough what he had done, though not by any intention of his own, which is why I absolved him then and there.

Dearest Mother,

As I hope you won't mind my addressing you, since I know that if you were to reply to my letters, as I know you cannot, I am sure that you would call me child or, better still, daughter, for which I would disclaim my forsakenness, I surely would — I beg your forgiveness for this long delay caused, you may be sure, by a catastrophe that well justifies such a lapse in my duty.

The old man has died. Mrs. Evelyn Stack's father, that is, and the event has thrown us all, babies and animals included, into a period of protracted commiseration in which you cannot hear the church bells for the sound of our grieving. Mrs. Stack has postponed for the time her reading and lecturing to the children, though I confess that in the valley of my night, as I know it to be, and on the sly, though I regret having to say the phrase, I have been reading to myself Mrs. Stack's prized tome about the Irish prince who, if I may say so, does a great deal more than become a bishop, since there is a glorious girl in the tale who changes everything.

The poor old creature died outside, as you would have expected, tending as usual his affliction, so at least he was found with the old horse nudging his corpse, quite as if that aged horse had been a dog, a thought that had never occurred to me before and as strange as it was true.

Mrs. Evelyn Stack ordered her father laid out on the dining-room table beneath a crystal chandelier and formally adorned with numerous flowers, out of season the lot of them, and it was Corporal Stack who carried him in and arranged him properly and helped prepare the breads and cakes and meats and beer for the grievers, family and neighboring families from farms not nearly as grand as the Stack family's, and the feasting carried us through at least in going through the motions.

The burial itself was a lovely affair, with all gathered in the little yard behind the church I have alluded to already, and the rain holding off and Mrs. Stack's babies rolling about between the canted headstones as if they could not recognize the Stack family's austere history recorded on those lichen-covered stones, which of course they could not, and as if they had forgotten why we were there in that soft garden of solemnity in the first place, which alleviated our grief momentarily. I don't know what Evelyn, as Corporal Stack calls his cousin, would have done without the strength of character and sheer religious vigor of Corporal Stack, who gave her his arm and paid the priest and offered a eulogy for the dead and departed. Could I have been the only one present to see the old man's spirit making off faintly above the dampened treetops while the corporal spoke? I am not sure, but indeed I saw the old man fading from us on the rhythm of the corporal's words.

I have grown up nurturing the first mystery, the enigma that is every foundling's birthright, though I know full well that the church forbids this way of thinking and denies what I call the hollowness of our beginning. Now this death among us has introduced me to the second, and just as firmly renounced by our mother church, which causes me to say, no matter the sin of doing so, that there can be no first vacancy without the last, as you yourself well knew from the start and which does not contradict the spiritual teachings you have provided us. Oh, Foundling Mother, you see how fortuitous has been our visit to High Crosses of Kells, and how altered has become my mood. Oh, Mother, I shall never be a glorious girl and there's the end of it! But I know you will not despair for me as you shouldn't.

Without Teddy to read my letters, I had no choice but to handle that matter myself, though I could hear his every laugh and sneer yet made no changes though I knew he was right. So too I was forced to manage the posting, but at serious cost to my personal pride since the stableboy I was forced to engage was more demanding than even Mr. Lackey had been, and

I had already decided that I had had enough experience of that kind for my purpose and wanted no more, especially with Teddy injured and confined as he was. Nevertheless I paid the stableboy's price with hardly a word of objection and occupying my mind with thoughts of Red Eddie and Finnula Malloy, and for all that managed to remain as bodily pure as I thought, quite wrongly, that the young mistress of Great Manor must herself still be.

How, anyone of sense might ask, could a foundling girl lose the only man she had ever loved in her life, a condition that persisted to the end of it, when that selfsame man lay somewhere within the very house in which that same young girl worked and worried and lay awake at nights? And yet the truth of the matter is that lose him I surely did from the moment George and William carried him off. The sixteen-year-old who was the blonde Miss to my poor You turned me over to Mary Grant, who cooked and managed the place and cared for the babies. Babies? Yes indeed, as if the foundling I was and the infants I invented in my letters to my own Mrs. Jennings were to ensure that never would I be free of the eternally begotten proof of the emptiness that so strives to fill our minds and hearts, and with reason.

Of course I heard the automobile going off for the doctor and tried to rush outside after it, to no avail. Of course I heard its return and tried again to thrust myself into their midst, to no avail, and had no better luck than to catch that young mistress off her guard and to beg the merest word or two of solace regarding Teddy, and to be denied. Constantly denied. At least I knew that Teddy lived, since the doctor continued to be fetched and returned to the village of which he was the sole center of comfort against the invisible, as those villagers knew full well, and justly proud of the fact too, though he came and went for sure with decreasing frequency.

So why did I not leave my cold room in the night and search out the entirety of Great Manor until I found my

Teddy where he must have been sleeping in coziness and warmth as well? The dogs, of course. I never knew their numbers, but I had only once to hear them growling at me in concert to retreat on my bare feet as swiftly as possible and, in tears and loneliness, to admit my defeat. Occasionally I saw one of them or perhaps the same dog more than once, and the evident brutality of the creature convinced me that this was no Irish hound but an animal imported from the wilds of some far-off land, as I later learned was true.

At least I was in the same house as was Teddy. At least the girl mistress of Great Manor had not carried him off while I lay awake listening for the faint sound that would betray the disaster I most dreaded. At least I had the reassurance of furtive glimpses of

141

the doctor with his pipe and bag, and eventually I began to hear Teddy's own voice from the furthest reaches of that awful house, which wrung my heart and left me more helpless and lovelorn than ever. For now I was the prisoner that I had never been while living in the Home for Foundling Girls in Carrickfergus, or even in Lackey's Livery Stable, where the forces beyond me had first assaulted my selfhood which, however, was still standing me in good stead, though sorely tried.

My domain, in which I counted for little no matter the sweat I poured into my work from morn to night, was the kitchen, as anyone might have known, and that single room was larger than kitchen and dining hall combined back at Saint Martha's, with an enormous hearth at one end and a battery of stone sinks at the other. A few iron stoves and then several long work-tables were situated beneath an iron contraption from which hung in menacing rows the knives and axes with which we went at the beef and lamb and various kinds of fowl with the fury known only to those long accustomed to serving on a kitchen staff. But why, I wanted to know from the first, why were we cooking such great quantities of meat and vegetables that kept us working in that hot oily place until I for one was ready to drop and every day too? Who, I wanted to know, could possibly consume the pots and platters that we prepared day in, day out, without a moment of peace to let the blood dry on the chopping blocks and the sweat on our faces?

And what about the infants? Her little bare brood as Mary Grant referred to them? First of all I did not realize that there were other living and breathing persons beside ourselves in Mary Grant's kitchen the day I was introduced to it, or consigned to it as I might say, since no sooner was I given over to Mary Grant, fear and bafflement still gripping me as they surely were, than I was set to work plucking and disemboweling a goose that would have made two of any goose that Mrs. Jennings roasted for our table back at Saint Martha's. Feathers, then, and slipperiness and splatterings while Mary Grant loomed here and there and I felt increasingly the fool for the ineptitude that my domestic education at Saint Martha's in no way justified, yet there it was.

Of course I had hardly caught my bearings, as Teddy used to say, except to know that I was in Great Manor, or in the servants' wing of Great Manor properly speaking, when I learned for myself the extent and grandness of this old family house. And noted the broken windows here and there that no one, least of all a foundling in my predicament, could have predicted. Vandals, I told myself. For shame. Yet why should vandals from wherever, and however few, come out of the night to aim their rocks at such a nice old place? — though surely it was the strangest and most disagreeable place in which I had ever found myself, alas. And my inability to answer the question, which made the more unsatisfactory my effort to do so, only added to the perversion — that was the only word for it — that hung down upon Great Manor like a stench on a bog. And of course I had not even removed my hat, as the saying goes, before having been put to work on a goose that daunted my spirit, I can tell you. And of course and mainly there was Teddy, or rather there was not Teddy, at least for me. In the midst of all this, and despite Mary Grant and her silence and largeness and uncomfortable closeness to me as I plucked away at the fierce resistance of that goose's feathers, I began to have intimations of life or at least movement in the peculiar heap of rugs and rags piled up beside the hearth in the warmth of its smoky fire.

Pluck I did, the while avoiding as best I could the wicked black beak that would have taken my hand off, given half a chance, no matter that the wretched bird was dead, yet noticing that that curious heap of cast-off cloth by the hearth was moving, shifting here and there with a life of its own, until I saw the little tin feeding dishes and turned back to my goose with a smile. Cats, I told myself. Dogs. Or kittens or pups. But then it came to me that the way the rags and rugs or perhaps old pieces of quilts or blankets were shifting about was more suggestive of a nest of mice, which gave me dreadful pause, I can tell you. Then, forgetting the goose altogether, I could not help but stare straight on because a tiny hand and then an arm protruded, accompanied by other little hands and arms protruding in the exact same way, until the babies, for such they were indeed, began poking and crawling forth from the hive, as I may call it, of old clothes and blankets and useless rags as if they had never before known the pangs of hunger or the warmth of light.

Oh, Mum, look at the poor things!

Whereupon the old ogress, which I knew her to be by the size and color of the warts on her face and hands, asked me if I had never seen an infant in my life — me, of all the girls in the world! and infants! infants, she asks me! — and went on to admit that she took them in, as she put it, and was known throughout the country round for asking no questions and taking them in, this charity, as I supposed it was, winning me over a bit to Mary Grant yet only fueling the more my inability to make any sense of Great

Manor and the life therein.

As for the tin dishes, I was right in my first surmise, for no sooner did the infants emerge and start their mewling and puling and blind feeling about, though most of them could see as well as their eyes allowed and as well as those babes safely institutionalized like most of us, than Mary Grant stooped down with considerable com-plaining of breath and took away the dishes and filled them, and then let in the dogs or rather pups as I should say. I managed well enough to contain my horror at the appearance of the sloppy and slathering young dogs, thinking of the harm they could do the infants, though most of the pups had as yet no teeth. In fact I was grateful to have my attention fully diverted to the babies, when suddenly Mary

Grant began scooping them up by the armful, as it seemed to me, and popping them on and off her bosom, at the same time indicating that I was to assist the larger of the children in eating their gruel, which indeed I did and with a good deal of relief, despite the fact that one of the little creatures was sorely ill, as I could tell by her eyes and her near inability to eat, no matter what I cooed to her while holding the spoon. This was little Martha, as I might have known.

Then back to the goose.

Before I went up to my room at the end of that first day and just as dusk was upon us, I was able to slip outside for a turn around Great Manor and the grounds, a practice I enjoyed that day and the rest to come, as much as I could enjoy anything at Great Manor, despairing as I did for Teddy, and my feelings of distress at my dislocation, no matter the solace of the infants who slept all together or kept getting underfoot in a most unconventional manner. Dusk, then, and I slipped from tree to tree, hugging myself or wringing my hands, and always spying upon Great Manor. There it was, like an abandoned ship on a knoll, it was that large and had been built on the only high ground as far as I could see, excepting, of course, the mountains that gave the distant horizon a nasty look of jaggedness. From behind whichever tree I was hiding, I looked for a lighted window, and saw a few, though the shattered glass in the darkest and coldest of those windows was so bright and clear to see that it might have cut my fingers. I saw almost nothing of anyone inside, for all my spying. Sometimes, in days to come, I took myself to the kitchen garden and marveled at the extent of the produce thick and lovely in the evening dew. But for whom was this vast garden cultivated? It was a sumptuous sight, to say the least, but unreasonable, like everything that concerned Great Manor.

Flee! I counseled myself that first evening, run for help! But I had sense enough to abandon the thought and calm myself and make my way back to the kitchen, where, in half darkness, Mary Grant gave me an unpleasant look and led me up to the crookedness of the back stair. On the bed was a nightdress no servant had ever worn in her life, though clearly it was a cast-off garment and now mine.

Dear Foundling Mother,

This time, I fear, the contents of my letter shall be nearly as short as my salutation. Misfortune — one of the direst kind — has descended upon the heads of the Stack family and for what sins of the distant past I cannot imagine. The house is blighted, as it appears to me. For no sooner had we bid farewell to poor old Mr. Stack senior, with all possible respects both in the home itself and in the church and then in the little enduring churchyard as I have described, than one of Evelyn Stack's homeless children came down with a fever that surely would have carried her off had it not been for Evelyn Stack's own presence of mind, which so far has proven as good as a suit of armor against the dark wayward clouds of death and the unknown. And now, when the sick child is not entirely out of danger, Corporal Stack himself has become the unwilling host to that poor child's fever. He lies abed, Mum, mere walls and generations from the little one, now waning, now reviving, and as you will be the first to know, the miasma that enrobes the child is far more lethal in the grown man, or potentially so. The baby is sick, Corporal Stack is sicker, and crying out to his men in the trenches to don their respirators and advance.

Oh, Mum, while the poor soldiers of Corporal Stack's delirium climb from their trenches and go forth, I remain all the more mired in assisting Evelyn to care for our own patients, and the time of my return is receding. . . .

There, I thought, was truth enough that Teddy himself might not have objected as strenuously as usual, and truth enough that I would not have cared had he done so. It was with the cautious delivery of this letter to the stableboy that I began to regard with greater appreciation that boy's simpleness of soul. His name was Micka and he claimed to have come into this world from the womb of a mare — a foolish idea to which nonetheless I lent a curious credence.

Then to the candle. Then to sleep. And wondering would I ever be myself again in that nightdress.

How cold they were, those first

nights I spent in my abandoned corner of Great Manor, safe as I supposed yet captive too, and knowing that I was not clothed in sinful luxuriance for nothing. Of course I could not sleep for thinking of Teddy and hearing the sounds of laughter and voices and a musical instrument in some far-off room where those menacing dogs must have been drowsing at the feet of their young mistress. And the wind, such a welcome visitor to Great Manor, went up and down in the vastness of the place, pausing now here, now there, then whistling on like some infernal breath from Evelyn Stack's majestic book of Irish tales, though neither the woman or the book existed, as occasionally I was forced to remind myself. Those were the nights when I should have dropped off at

once when darkness became conclu-
sive and I was freed to climb alone to
my room, more oppressed than I had
ever been in my life and as exhausted,
surely, as some country woman of
great age worn out with working. But
I did not and only lay there in a bed
so empty, as it had been for that long
that no sleeper's body could have
warmed it, let alone a young girl's alert
in uncertainty, and tried to protect
myself for Teddy's welfare and the
helplessness of my predicament by
wondering what Finnula Malloy
would have done in my stead. Finnula
would have made sweet work of
Micka, that was a certainty, and in
truth there was no reason why I
should not do the same, except for my
upbringing and my resolutions about
keeping myself for Teddy — and still

I was cold, and the bed was cold and Great Manor was coldest of all by nature and through and through. Thus hugging my own thin shoulders as if I might have been some other poor shivering girl, I gave myself over to worries and the imponderable, against which even the bodily heat of Finnula Malloy as I invented it, went cold.

She is sick, Mum. What can we do?

And who are you to think she's any different from the rest?

Nobody, Mum.

And what do you know about sickness in babies?

Nothing, Mum.

Well then, don't draw my attention to that infant. They're all the same and no one of them is sicker than the rest.

Oh, but Mrs. Grant, I am worried!

Have you not paid attention? You have not the station in life to be worried. Look to yourself, such as you are, and leave the worries to your betters.

If you say so, Mum.

But Mrs. Grant was wrong, or partially so, as the terrible days bore out, and soon I began to regret my part in the continued duping of my unsuspecting Foundling Mother, for already the similarity between what came unbidden onto the sheet of paper and what was now happening to me and, as I assumed, to Teddy, was becoming all too evident, as I could not help but see, as if I had only to hear her words in my head to find myself awakening to some new dread event as familiar to me as my own hand. Was I the cause? Was I the effect? But of what, I asked myself, as if I had not troubles enough at Great Manor, with more to come.

If the kitchen was my domain, as it truly was, nonetheless it was I who was soon sent to gather the eggs and work in the garden with a wooden spade and to pick berries from the bushes that sprawled untended and thus near wild about the grounds, all of which established clearly enough that the young mistress had no fear that I would run off, which in light of what had happened was reasonable enough, and which in truth meant that

I was my own captor or at least collaborator in my confinement. Even by my second day at Great Manor I lost track of time, or so it seemed, and found myself overburdened as even the fittest of farm girls was never likely to be. Rushing about from angry bush to angry hens nesting in outbuildings dank and rotten-smelling from the decay with which they were infected increasingly from year to year, and then inside and cooing to little Martha, poor thing, my worries about the child growing daily, and then out again to gather into my bare arms the carcass of one of our slaughtered sheep that single-handedly I was meant to roast — thus the demands that had been put upon me were in themselves insurmountable barriers against my finding Teddy. And on top of everything I was soon required to fill the varied roles of domestic inside Great Manor and in halls and chambers far beyond the kitchen.

Yet within mere days of my arrival I found a hiding place in which I could pause a moment and try to be myself, taking heart from its natural beauty and freed from the fears that so overwhelmed me in my cold bed at night. It was beneath a bridge, unlikely though such a declaration sounds. In point of truth, at a certain distance from Great Manor, but not beyond the menacing mood of the place, which extended far, a small creek came winding along through the furze and it was this bit of dappled water that was crossed by a small stone vaulted bridge. Its span was short, it was wider than need be and rising in its center to a curiously high hump. Not only was it a dwarfed and ancient thing built of great rocks and blocks of stone older than Great Manor, as I surmised, but it was overspread with lichen and then smothered in ivy. Imagine!

True enough my bridge, as I thought of it when first I spied it down the knoll partially hidden in the glen, looked sore and scabrous from the lichen, and heavily hidden under its growths of ivy, and was a further instance of irrationality since the footpath it served was no longer used or even visible and the rivulet could easily be crossed in a step or two with only a few slips and wettings. But it was old, my misshapen bridge, and chunky, and so out of place and harmless, for all its malformations of various kinds, that I could not help but find it alluring at first sight. With no one to tell me and no book either, I knew at once that this was an Irish bridge, a monument to fierceness and olden times, a dark and sorry structure under which a girl as beset and lost as I was might find her shelter.

So I took to stealing down the hill when I could and hiding for a few moments each busy day, or most of them, beneath my bridge. The rock I sat upon was a comfort, wet or dry. The dark ferns were intricate and as small as my broken fingernail, the agitated trickle of water just beyond my toes was too cold to drag my fingers in but lovely to watch, and the darkness provided by the dripping arch overhead was natural and uncontaminated, as I wrongly thought.

Wrongly I say. Wrongly. For one afternoon as I was crouching beneath the bridge, cloaked to invisibility for sure by the ivy, I was startled to hear a footfall as heavy and ominous as any I might have dreaded to hear in the night. Then another. Slowly. Great brutish steps thumping one after another with a purpose I could not allow myself to divine and yet could not escape. Then breathing louder than the sound of the water. Then the impression of a large figure dressed in black, that of a man, and that I barely had time to see as all at once he was upon me stooping and catching hold of me and dragging me forth and up, into his arms or rather under one of them without a word or any sign of disapprobation, and carried me limp and fearing most the loss of my wits, back up to Mary Grant where she waited, hands on hips, and wanting to know what I thought I was doing, hiding myself away under that old bridge. The size of my captor, for he towered above Mrs. Grant, who was a large woman herself, and the anomalous way his formal clothing of black suit and white shirtfront contrasted with the stony shadowy niche in which I had been crouching, and above all the silence in which he apprehended me and snatched me up and carried me off without the slightest regard for my person, all left me quite bloodless and unable to talk until I was called upon to poke up the fire and tend to the bare brood.

Thus my introduction to Mr. Jakes. Later, softening somewhat, Mary Grant explained to me that every es-

tate house of the upper classes demanded its own manservant, or several perhaps, and that Mr. Jakes was
the only surviving "man," as such persons were sometimes called for short,
at Great Manor. She warned me that
since I knew nothing of social conduct
I must try the harder to acquire what
I could of deference, since Mr. Jakes
might require from me even more deference than did the young mistress. I
did not argue with Mary Grant, no
matter my immediate abhorrence of
whatever she wanted me to learn or
feel. And though she forbade me any
more stealing off to hide from herself
and my duties, I persisted in my occasional visits to the bridge, though
only after reassuring myself that Mr.
Jakes had retired for his daily rest. But
my hiding place had lost a certain fla-

vor of Irish tranquillity, thanks to him. I think I need say nothing of the furry wen on his neck.

From then on and as one might expect, I was beset by a new worry, which was that one night I should hear the proud immensity of Great Manor's only manservant coming up the crookedness of the back stair. I might have spared myself that particular source of wakefulness since it was not like Mr. Jakes to harm me in any such obvious manner, as I should have known from our episode at the bridge, despite the wen on his neck.

Soon thereafter my duties were extended, as I have already said, from kitchen and gardens and infants and squawking birds whose deaths I became proficient at inflicting, and without assistance, to the private halls and chambers of Great Manor's vast and, I always felt, forbidding interior. I started to learn the location of the rooms that were inhabited and the rooms that were only meant to be but were kept ready, and the kitchen bells whose ringing was infallible, which is to say that they hung in a row on a board and were numbered, so that if number 21 rang, for instance, the meaning was that a servant was wanted without doubt in the corresponding room, presuming that we on the household staff knew which room was which, since of course they had no numbers. No painted numbers, that is. So I had no choice but to follow after Mr. Jakes, comparing his unwholesome bulk to Mr. Canty's, as indeed I had never forgotten it, from Canty's Pub of course, or to Major

Minford's, despite the disappointment he had caused me, the while thinking pointedly of my own Corporal Stack, who was by no means manly in any conventional way but was nonetheless dear to me as the others weren't and who surely lay alive and perhaps improving in one of the rooms that Mr. Jakes was teaching me to know.

Never did I follow Mr. Jakes with deference. But never did a young girl try harder to learn to identify some far-off room with the sudden ringing of a little bell. It was not easy. And wouldn't you know but that all those bells in that kitchen row were rusted through and through as with the passage of time and disuse? How then could they ring so sharply and so often, jolting me upright from what-

ever task I might be bent to, and sum-
moning me off to some empty room
that foxed my memory good and
proper and thwarted my smallest
thought of usefulness? Oh, it was a
situation of anxiety and frustration, I
can tell you. Of course I was com-
pelled to do my duty, whatever it was,
as I had learned at Saint Martha's, and
quickly too and without thinking, and
of course I was frantic to repossess the
oldest soldier alive in Saint Clement's,
as I thought of him to keep up my
spirits. So when one of those sharp
bells drove me to the wrong room,
which I did not allow to happen often,
I was in despair and thrashed my ineptitude good and proper, figuratively
speaking. And when the call I answered was the correct one, which it
sometimes was, I found it difficult to

conceal my pleasure or to keep my eyes on the tray I carried and not stop on the threshold and allow my eyes to look about that enormous room eagerly, even when I knew full well that Teddy was not there.

Oh, but I was vulnerable to more than the exasperating bells for sure. As on the day when Mr. Jakes informed me that I would be serving tea that afternoon. For hours I tried to prepare myself, too proud to ask either Mr. Jakes or Mary Grant just what would be expected of me when I carried in the tray too large for me to hold safely or comfortably, with the little bone china cups rattling and the tea scalding as I discovered when I tried to lift the pot. But for some reason or lack of reason neither Mr. Jakes, seated in the shadows in a corner, nor Mary Grant, who loaded the tray, offered a word of advice or encouragement, as if they quite enjoyed my predicament and were indifferent to their own contributions to the deterioration of Great Manor's staff. There was cake, there were kippers, there was an immense bowl of boiled eggs soft in the middle, and rashers of bacon that was mainly fat and hence a treat for anyone trying to survive in our nation, native-born or not.

The passageways from kitchen to parlor were long and many, and cold too, and empty, and littered with tiny rugs from far-off lands as it seemed to me and curling at the edges and prone to sliding any which way beneath my step, so that trying to accommodate the necessary haste required to reach the parlor with the tea still warm, as

well as the eggs and cakes and sandwiches, demanded the greatest possible risk of me and enrobed me in fear
and treachery before I had even
reached the presence of those who
would presumably devour the opu-
lence I strove to carry. And few they
were too.

Oh, Thistle. Just put down the tray
on this table. I'll do the pouring.

As you say, Miss.

At least she called me by a name I
recognized, though coming from her
and in that situation it was just as
humiliating as her usual You, though
truth be told I saw her infrequently
enough and a good thing too, which
is what I told myself in self-protection.
And was it easy to put down the tray
as she had instructed me to do in that
lighthearted and totally false voice of

hers? It was not. I was distracted, you see, by the feeble little fire on the old blackened hearth that could have accommodated a goodly blaze by the size of it. And also by the mistress of Great Manor herself, who wore fresh hunting clothes and was standing with her back to the fire like a man and not a young woman prettier than I and more mature though about my height, as I had to admit within the little privacy still mine, and as thin as I too, and also by the young man seated on a little gilded chair that would surely collapse beneath him before I could rid myself of the terrible unsteady burden I tried to hold outstretched and steer and around which I could not see and would drop if startled by the heavyset young man whose horrible expression was the exact opposite from and hence the perfect mate to the young mistress's thin smile. The very weight of that tray had almost reached the heaviness that I must in a moment drop, even in silence and disregarding the great chair made of dried-out leather and as large as a wardrobe and directly facing the fire so that I had no view of its occupant except for a dangling arm and hand I thought I recognized with a gasp, as the eggs and the rest of it began to slide. When just in time she stepped forward and seized the great mass of thorns and silver, the tray that is, and a tiny flame shot up on the hearth.

Just tea and cake, Mlud? As usual?

Whereupon I made my temporary escape, though it could just as well have gone the other way and landed me on my hands and knees in disaster, and though even as I turned I was still trembling from the strain of the ordeal and the phantom weight of the tray.

You may go now, Thistle.

Thank you, Miss.

But no curtsy. I can tell you that. And this was not the only example of my vulnerability as I have said or at least implied. Such as the courage I was forced to summon every time I passed the old one-horned goat tethered at the far end of the kitchen garden, an immense maddened creature larger even than Cooky had been and who saw in every living thing, even a poor Irish foundling like myself, the brute who had broken off more than half of the horn that was missing, leaving only one good horn and a stub atop his bony head. Not to mention the fury of the heavens and the dogs and my inability to please Mary Grant or to keep from dropping things, knives or kettles, when one of the rusted bells rang out — and without warning, as they always did. Sometimes, when I was not at my spading, say, the young mistress would startle me by appearing from nowhere and suddenly saying aloud my name, softly, coming at me in goodwill, and bidding me tramp the nearer hills as her companion, which I could not help but do, holding my ears while she brought down this small bloodied bird or that one with a firearm that had once belonged to her daddo. And who but me for finding and fetching the little shattered carcasses that dropped like stones and always hid themselves good and proper in thorny thickets that even one of her ravenous hounds would have found impenetrable? Exactly, since on all those jaunts we were never accompanied by one of those hounds, as reason would have dictated, which would have increased my fear and perplexity tenfold at the least. But even from within those thickets and for all the world imprisoned, as it would come to me, the sight of her through the thorns when she thought I was not looking, made me admit to myself that she was a willowy proud girl and lovely to see. Her long face was as thin as my own and the lips were unnaturally full as from a habit of biting them on cold days, as I decided. When I crawled out, thrusting away the dead birds into an old leathern sack that had once belonged to her daddo's man, as she also said, did I not suddenly find her looking at me with what, at Saint Martha's, would have been recognized at once as love in her eyes? I did. And briars and thorns were nothing to me for that rare look in her eyes.

One afternoon she appeared in the kitchen unannounced and took me aback, exactly as might have one of the long-suffering bells or Mr. Jakes himself, gliding up to me for some sinister purpose I could never fully see in the dark, my sight going blank, so to speak, when the barest thought of him intruded. She entered unseen and unforeseen and addressed me as You and told me to follow her and bring a chair. It took only that to overcome me once again in my fear and dislike of her, wondering what she could possibly want and why she was a person of such vagrancy of spirit and I so constantly and in a certain light pathetically unchanging — willing and open-minded, that is, as I had learned to be from our own Mrs. Jennings, perhaps to my disadvantage as I often thought. Yet I would have myself no other way as I knew, except in instances like the present one when I was near to having no self at all. By the time I was able to carry the chair outside, she was already off through the slowly collapsing arbor and into a protective square of hedge grown wild, and waiting, and smiling, I was relieved to see. Then, taking the chair and handing me a silver comb and a pair of thin silver scissors with blades as long and sharp as one of Mary Grant's sharpest kitchen knives, she told me that I was to cut her hair, which at first I declined to do, for obvious reasons, though secretly pleased that she entrusted to me so intimate an operation. Then what do you know but she stripped off her shirt and sat down in the chair, though I was hardly able to keep my wits about me at the sight of her, and in passing failed to catch any connection between partial nakedness and haircutting, which she did not bother to explain. But she prevailed, of course, by speaking kindly and coaxing me with gentle words I had never thought to hear from the likes of Teddy's abductor, which she had come to be, and displaying only her usual indifference though her chest was bare.

There she sat in the sunlight the way she did on a horse, straight in her slender back and sure of herself, with all her hardness of manner sloughed away as with the shirt on the ground, and her strength of mind concealed within a girlhood that was suddenly like mine, difference in age or no difference in age. And there I stood, unfamiliar comb and scissors filling my hands with the unbearable fact that I did not even know which way to hold them and trying to keep myself from looking at her bare brightness from the belt up, which I could not do. Of course I had seen the naked likes of myself in Saint Martha's, though exactly how long ago I could no longer determine, and yet there was no comparison, really, between all those girls trying to catch each other's bodies in the washup time and the sight of the young mistress of Great Manor sitting still as she was and that close to me and the sunlight hardly daring to touch her skin, her white and slightly rounded shoulders, and her chest too, driving home to me our scant though crucial difference in age, as I had to admit in the silence. Her blonde hair hung crookedly to her shoulders, leaving her chest uncovered, of course, and I could smell her unkempt hair and unclean shiny skin with its blue lines and ripples and even the anatomical girlishness fresh on her chest, which of course kept drawing my eyes as must have been only too apparent to the young mistress of Great Manor. My cheeks were warm and the young mistress's upper half of her body was warm too, thanks to the hesitant touch of that lovely sun. In the wild hedge all the tiny concealed birds had ceased their peeping and chirping at the sight of us, or rather at the sight of the young mistress, who must have known that she resembled a marble bust in a garden, except for her ragged shanks of long hair. It was in this suspended moment, as it were, that a quick glimpse of her face confirmed my earlier suspicion that even the young mistress of Great Manor bit her lips, which was why they were split-looking and unnaturally plump and of the special color they were. Was it possible that I, at a mere thirteen years of age, was on the verge of leaning in for a still closer look at her mouth and chest as well at the very instant that she reminded me of our purpose and the sound of her voice startled the little wild birds once more into disbelieving song and chatter? True enough, for such was I doing when she told me that I should put the comb in my apron pocket, for now, and with the scissors trim around her hair so that it hung clear of her shoulders, using my other hand, of course, to lift each hank of hair free for the blades. I obeyed, as how could I not? And for sure became the victim of opposing emotions when I first felt the sensation of her soft hair in my fingers and brought myself to apply the scissors and see a swatch of her unwashed hair fall loose.

Snip and falling, snip and falling, and so it went as I became more sure of myself but nonetheless cut her hair shorter and more unevenly with each application of the blades. Oh, and wasn't I set happily adrift, so to speak, by the clicking of the bright blades and the sight of her ears that would not have been allowed to remain in that condition for even a day at Saint Martha's? I was. Indeed I was. And the hair fell and the shadows fell and in grand style I worked my way round the half-naked mistress of Great Manor from her left side to her right, feeling the cold touch of her skin beneath my fingers and seeing a little place she had scratched and wisps of hair falling and floating off though there was no breeze. Her long neck came increasingly into view. My own breath stirred the short new baby hair beneath the hair I was clipping. Once more the birds stopped their singing. She licked her poor puffy lips. And there. I was done.

Silence was ours. Deservedly.

So I took a deep breath and stepped round to face her full front and admire my handiwork, so to speak, when without a word she reached out a hand for the scissors, which slowly and despite myself I gave her, and then still without a word she reached out the other and it took me a good long moment to recollect the comb, which I finally did.

Then she stood up and said that it was my turn. That it was only proper that we exchange places. That I bare myself as she had done and sit on the chair as she had done, and that she become the barber, so to speak, that I had been. Which was all very well, except that I was blushing in a way I did not wish to acknowledge, but there it was, brightening my face with the temptation to which in another moment or two of silence I would surely yield, and except — and here was the exception that most mattered — except that in that gaping luxurious silence she called me unwittingly by name. Not Thistle as she was wont to do every now and then. But Dervla. The Christian name that had been given to me by my own Foundling Mother, that is. Dervla, I heard her say. Dervla, in passing. Which by the mere sound of it swept away the entire scene of our breathlessness and set me running, that's for sure, helped along by those twin sisters of joy and rebellion. Behind me I heard her laughing as if she did not know what had got into me or what her thoughtless use of my truly given name had told me, or as if running off could make any difference, as indeed and gloomily seemed the case once I had reached Great Manor and the safety of my cold room. Whatever determination had shot me off that way was gone by the time I stood quivering at my window and through the masses of ivy saw her strolling back with the shirt hooked by a finger across one shoulder.

Like the girl she was. Like the lad she often seemed to be. Proud, furious, sweet as the hay. One minute matronly and the very next as forlorn as the rest of us, and I never knew which or when. But at least she had revealed what she could not have learned except from Teddy, come to his senses or still out of them, which I thought the likelihood since he had made no effort yet to seek me out and take me away forever from Great Manor.

Dear Foundling Mother,

Above the Stack farm there was a rent in the clouds! Healthy air has once again filled the house! We are safe, the lot of us!

You see, Mum, Corporal Stack has recovered, or nearly so, and sits in the new sunlight sipping broth or black tea and smiling at those of us who nursed him through. And the same may be said in its own terms of the little child now standing timidly among its tiny mates or taking warm milk from a bottle on Evelyn Stack's lap or mine. Relapsing does not seem in store for either man or child, thank goodness.

Mrs. Stack — Evelyn as I increasingly called her since I have been behaving more like an adult than a child and have been her stalwart companion in trying times — Mrs. Stack as I am quite content to call her now with the passing of the crises we have faced together, has returned to her long hours of reading aloud to all of us recovering health and good spirits, whether we are assembled around her or scattered throughout the house as new life demands. I hear her fine strident voice, and so does Corporal Stack and all the children spared what one of them nearly died of, especially that smallest girl who came so close to the darkness of the eternal light. Usually Mrs. Stack gathers her loved ones around her for the benefit of the uplifting words she reads, but now she reads aloud for herself if need be, knowing that all of us will hear the sounds of her instructive voice wherever we might be at the time. But who among us can refuse the clarity of her lofty voice and fail to draw near?

The tale of the young prince destined to be bishop of all the land, and of the young woman quite his equal in size and bearing and manner and mind too, has progressed through a goodly number of pages since my last letter, and through many adventures as well. They are Irish, of course, this immense young man and equally immense young woman who is always there to provide the saving blow of the sword or the cleverness that frees the prince from the evil in which he is forever getting himself ensnared, and by now it is clear that without this very same young woman the handsome prince would never have become our first bishop. Yes, she it was who never failed to be at the bishop's side through all his days of grandeur and the sacred life of our church, though of course, dear Foundling Mother, Mrs. Stack has not gotten quite so far in the story.

I think that Corporal Stack will be ready to return to Carrickfergus much sooner than I understandably thought when he lay abed as in the mud and fire of the war in which he would have given his life had it been needed, and when Mrs. Evelyn Stack spent hours kneeling at his bedside praying that he be spared in her own home as he had been spared with his men who of course were not so fortunate.

I scrub myself clean each dawn and dusk, needless to say, and hourly miss your firm smile and the clarity you instill into all our lives at

Saint Martha's.

Be sure, Mum, to save my letters.

Micka received his due for dispatch-
ing this one, which nearly caused me
to break my vows. How then, I asked
myself, could any girl wait three years
for what he described to me in the
stable? And why must I, when surely
Finnula Malloy would not? And in
fact did not as I came to learn in time.

So in the dark of every night I pon-
dered my situation in which my beginning felt to me trapped in its own
end, or worse still the other way
round. Had the clock stopped or was
it merely winding down? I would listen to the very cold of the place and
with my own hands feel about my bed
to be sure that I was its only occupant,

which was both good and bad.

Where was Teddy? Was he lying awake in the dark as I was and thinking of me as I was of him? Despite his great age, that was quite beyond reckoning as I believed, and his bravery proven by the stories he told, and the way he had of resembling no man and of savoring his superiority in the face of adversity and fellows who admitted that they were no match for him — despite all this, I asked myself, was he nonetheless lying awake with only me in his mind? I hoped he was. I called upon the higher powers to grace us both in the way I was asking. Yet I knew it was not so, no matter what the higher powers had in mind for us. For as it had come to me on a day I could no longer remember, if Teddy was in full possession of his wits he would have let nothing stand between us a moment longer, or as long as it takes the birds to start up their singing at the first light. So somewhere, then, he was raving or whispering my name or saying it but without quite making sense, or saying nothing at all and smiling, which amounts to the same thing, while it was left to me to be clear in my head but do nothing, because I could not for everything else I was doing. Oh, he was more of a person than I was, and though he was mine in spirit as I had known from the start, yet here I was alone and quite unable to act for myself let alone the two of us, and thus be true to the character that Mrs. Jennings had been the one to see in me so early on. But I could not. If I could have been my own Thistle then wouldn't I have been his Dervla? But I could not, as I was forced to admit to myself each night, though in my long daily hours of what would have amounted to indenture had there been an end in sight, I did my best to serve them, for that was the kind of girl I was too, while trying as I might to be my own person, which was the very person I most feared was fading, yet of course was the very person on whom Teddy and I both depended.

So there they were, every night a snarl, so to speak, in which I clung to Teddy and clung to myself and fell into sleep in search of common sense and the powers to be heroic, which I knew were not mine.

How long could I resist the importunings of Micka, though he was only a lad and younger than myself as well?

How many more letters could I afford to write?

Stand firm, I admonished myself throughout those days. No complaining. But in point of fact I would not have complained even had there been a person, any person, to hear me out and comfort my head on her bosom. But there was not. I could rely on nothing, I knew, except on my own compliance and duplicity, and for the most part I could no longer tell which was which and did not care. It was only in my mind that I avoided Mr. Jakes, yet I knew nonetheless that I was not deceiving him. I set my face so as not to allow the young mistress to see that I knew what I had done to her hair, and tried to conceal my shame whenever she passed, though well or ill was not mine to know. There were days when I was convinced that the goat had broken his chain, or that little Martha, who had taken to standing beside my chair in the kitchen whenever I was not heeding the bells or serving tea, a prospect I no longer found quite so fraught with agony, was appealing to me as clearly as if she had all at once acquired speech, which she had not, to do something and to help her and to cool down her fever as if I had had the doctor's skills or character enough to persuade Mrs. Grant to heed my worries and act accordingly. None of which I was able to do, yet hardly stopped thinking of the miserable child throughout the day, when I never knew from whatever quarter they might be having at me. And if I managed to find a little heart, as I knew I must, why along would come another one of their blows to my spirit, as they surely were, from behind a door or jumping at me in an empty room.

Why, for instance, could I not have had admittance to the private chapel, which was little enough to ask as it seemed to me? It was true that Mrs. Grant one day explained to me, without my asking, that every family in the landed gentry, as were the inhabitants of Great Manor, servants excluded, as she said, must by ancient custom have its own private chapel, which I thought a marvelous idea to say the least. But why could I not have a look inside and amaze myself or console myself without anyone knowing? Why, in other words, was that little stone chapel locked up as tight as it was and the key lost? Because, said Mrs. Grant, the young mistress had no particular interest in worship, and because it had been consecrated to a persuasion that was not ours, whatever Mrs. Grant could have meant by such a statement. Yet weren't there times when in the silence of the kitchen bells I heard the chapel bell faintly ringing the Angelus and went to the window and saw the landed gentry, all three of them, walking in slow procession out to their chapel, where their own private priest was waiting? There were indeed such times, and many too, during which times I understood how fortunate I had been among the other girls in the back of the church in Carrickfergus when I for one had not appreciated what was going on up at the altar. Of course I knew full well that my nostalgia for the past that was not entirely lost to me was a severe threat to clearheadedness, and that I must not indulge my feelings about the ivy-covered chapel for very long at a time if I was to preserve my mind and rescue Teddy too.

So I would tear myself from the window and finish my obligations in the kitchen and convince myself that I had not to worry about some peremptory summons from one of the kitchen bells and to set off to undertake my obligations in the library or parlor or study or the vast and windblown ballroom in which, according to Mrs. Grant, there had once been orchestras and dancing. Early on I felt considerable trepidation upon proceeding alone into such halls and corridors that filled Great Manor, but then with experience I went about my duties with a certain cheer, since it is not given to every Irish foundling to send up a sudden cloud of moths from draperies hanging in tatters from ceilings as high as the trees in the forests or to straighten family portraits hanging forever askew on walls that were actually covered in leather, and mildewed too. From the broken windows, especially prevalent in the ballroom, came the smell of the Irish air outside, while within and all about me lay the odors of pipe smoke long dead and gone and of the ashes I was expected to remove from the parlor hearth when the three of them were not drinking their tea and chatting. Sometimes I was tempted to sit down in the little gilded chair, since it was more appropriate to my slight weight than to the hulk of the young master, for such he was, but even this mean pleasure I denied myself.

Soon I detected the smell of drink in the parlor.

Of course it must have been there all along, fainter or stronger according to circumstances beyond my ken, and of course I had already been introduced to that festive aroma in Michael Canty's pub, when I had been offended by the antiseptic taint of its smell and yet delighted by its singular vigor that came as much from the drinkers as from the drink in their glasses. And what had I seen painted above the bar in Michael Canty's pub? Oh, yes indeed. *The Irishman eats English filth but thank God drinks Irish whiskey*, which is exactly how I would have put the matter had I been a man. But the parlor of Great Manor was hardly Michael Canty's pub or any other, and was certainly no place for drink. Furthermore, the smell I suddenly recognized on that particular occasion when I so wrongly assumed that I was alone in that fireless and hence inhospitable room, was nothing like the breath of life that had all but overcome me in Canty's Pub, but was sour and stale and noxious, though the bottle, when at last I saw it, was freshly opened and more than a third of it drunk too.

No flame on the hearth. No sound of voices. So in I came, thinking only that this was not the hour for tea and hence that I was safe once more or still, depending on one's view of the passing hours, and free to indulge my self-absorption and to busy myself at the tasks of the parlor maid I was trying to be. I could even have been humming to myself had my self-deception not been so fraught with danger, while with my back to the hearth I nonetheless felt the cold draft coming down into the room and saw the freshly accumulated dust on all the surfaces awaiting the deft touch of my rag. A veritable busybody for sure, giving a little bowl a quarter turn, just so, on the sideboard with the broken leg, and flicking the tip of my rag as if I had been dusting their treasures all my life. Then stopping short. Indeed I stopped short in my efforts and went rigid, the rag dangling from my cold fingers. Outside a poor bird landed against one of the windows partially concealed behind the dank drapes as cold and dead as winding sheets for sure, and I heard the thud and the silence of its sad fall. I listened. I sniffed. I took a deep inhalation. And again. Whiskey, I said to myself, and shivered as the import of that smell and word struck home. Slowly I turned, possessed and baffled as well, and in the instant saw the opened bottle on the tea table and, seated on the gilded chair, the heavyset young man slumping over the glass of whiskey in one of his thick hands. Had he not heard me enter? Was he not aware of my presence? Or was he just absorbed in his drinking and indifferent to a lowly girl who for him had no more life in her than the chair his increasing weight would in another moment send crashing into splinters of gold and remnants of faded gray fabric adorned with mournful roses dead on their stems? But why had I not seen the young master with my first step into that room in which he was entombed? Why not have smelled the whiskey at first breath of the cold close air in that parlor where the poor fellow sat alone drinking himself to death while waiting for his sister to light the fire? Who then the ghost? Himself or me?

Even while I watched, a bit of light came through a crack between the drapes and fell full on the bottle but deepened the shadows around the drinker slouching down in all the weakness of his tender bulk. That bit of sun lit up the golden drink remaining yet in the bottle and despite the shadows revealed as by some ancient artist the young master's pinkish hand and the glass it held. Beside him, as I saw as well, stood or rather leaned an old pair of hunting boots caked not only with dust but dried mud of the fields over which, I was certain, the young master himself had never ridden. Did he expect me to collect those boots without disturbing his recovery, a morbid state for sure, and carry them off for a good cleaning? Oh, those boots were quite as ghostly as himself. And I, perhaps because in the moment of seeing them I knew that their owner was long buried and gone, which did not much help my understanding of the perturbing scene, was once again an unwilling and unacknowledged actor both.

The light thickened about the bottle. The golden whiskey shone forth like a golden crown. The man groaned. Another bird fell to the ground outside. I took a timid step in his direction. One more. The fumes that came from the mouth of the bottle or the man's own mouth were noxious, as I have said, which I also failed to understand thanks to my memories of the warm and glowing aroma in Canty's Pub. And once more, drawing closer to that poor figure in the gilded chair despite myself.

When without the slightest warning the ax came down in the parlor of Great Manor.

Which is to say that there was a sound. And a tremor. And his fresh hand managing to return the shaking glass to the table and just in time, too. The tremor carried itself through all the beams and floors of the old place and, naturally, up through the very soles of my feet as well. I could not breathe. I could not stop my guilty and horrified staring at the enormous young man from whom, I realized, the sound was coming. With the greatest concentration he was able to draw his hand away from the golden glass and bottle without knocking them off the table, as I thought he must, but could do nothing about the sound or tremors as his great sad person glowed with his inability to save himself or house or me from what was swelling up inside him. But still he was valiant, slouching there in his hunting clothes, he who as far as I knew never once ventured as far as the stable, and mustering all his strength of character, which was not much, to keep down the convulsions which he must have suddenly realized were his and hence unavoidable, and with the sad white hand as big as a beast's paw reach out for the nearest of the old riding boots covered with the mud of centuries.

His face was red. He was his own boar at bay. And then he erupted and heaved and gagged, with the roof beams cracking and Great Manor resounding to the terrible sound of his retching. Oh, it was a deep sound, a dark and uncontrollable sound, an inward and outward bellowing such as I had never heard. Did he mean to blow himself apart from within, poor man? And would it never stop, this rumbling and desperation that I began to think that neither he nor I could possibly survive?

But it did. We did.

His bloated red face turned white, the booming sound of him diminished. Slowly the contractions grew less intense, less frequent, until from the young master, thoroughly haggard by now, there came only an intermittent watery sound as of some great torrent dying down to a trickle. Then silence. Then at last the reassurance that it was over, and my inaudible sigh of relief as I saw him slowly set down the boot without spilling its contents, though there was nothing he could do about the smell.

As for me, I turned as pale as the young master and suddenly thought to thank the blessed powers for providing the boot, without which my own lowly fate would have demanded — exactly. And even standing there in that stinking parlor I was not convinced that I would have been up to the task. But was I now expected to carry away the still warm and befouled

214

boot just as every dawn I carried out the chamber pots more numerous than those few lofty residents of Great Manor could possibly have required? But I would not. I would not. I would have nothing to do with it and turned, without even timidly offering the young master my assistance, and in the strength of my gathering pride fled the room, making not so much as a sound to disturb his misery.

Perhaps it was Mr. Jakes who disposed of the offensive boot, assuming that I had not been derelict in my duties but merely blind to that misplaced and misused boot in the parlor. At least it was not there when next I was required to serve them tea.

Adversities come to a person snout to tail as the young mistress herself once said, torn as she was between talking like a lad and a young woman of good manners, and mine were no exception, at least for as long as I was kept captive in Great Manor. For no sooner had I been forcibly exposed to the young master being sick to his stomach than they trapped and tormented me good and proper in the dining hall, and for all eyes to see. Oh, the roses may have bloomed and died between the day I saw the young master glass in hand and the day I was forced to serve Sunday dinner no less, I could not be sure. But as far as I knew nothing had changed, which is to say that Mrs. Grant's babies remained as small and pathetic as when I first saw them, though little Martha's illness worsened as I myself observed to Mrs. Grant, and the little infernal bells still rang. So it might as well have been the next day for all I knew, too busy as I was to care.

But I cared when Mrs. Grant informed me of what I was to be doing Sunday next. Indeed I did. Stopped dead where I was. Wiped the sweat from my brow. Talked back. Mustered courage enough to argue that I could not possibly do what she asked of me. Too young. Too shy. Too awkward. Except, as Mrs. Grant replied, she was not asking but telling, whereupon I wrung my hands and the babies set up a great howling and Mr. Jakes in his black suit and white shirt looked on from where he sat by the fire, that predatory manservant with his wen and his complacency, and with his walleye forever fixed on me.

How matter-of-factly Mrs. Grant had made her announcement. How it afflicted me in all the time that loomed between her informing me of the horror and the hour when it came to pass, though as I say there may not have been one honest day between the two. However long or short the intervening time, never in that period of waiting did I have a moment's relief from thinking of what lay in store for me. Oh, Mr. Jakes would prepare the table, with its heavy silverware and goblets, that much I knew, and Mrs. Grant would ready the roast, and perhaps the family so called would open their private chapel in which they might cleanse their souls and into which I might cast a furtive look before having to face the ordeal of serving a noontide Sunday dinner in Great Manor. It loomed before me, it lurked in cupboard drawers and corners, and gave me my own tremors at constantly having to imagine what I could not and yet would surely prove worse than all the eventualities that plagued me. What would I drop? What break? How disgrace myself in all their eyes and mine? The faster came these questions and attendant sights of myself on a day that had not even arrived, the more I occupied myself with the work that involved no willingness of mine nor predictability either, one day to the next. Now it was gathering eggs and breaking a round dozen, as I knew I would, and now it was setting off swiftly for the ballroom for I knew not what. And never a moment free of the impending event and the dread of it so strong as to efface my last hope of finding Teddy and taking him off — or nearly so. At the least I worried, on my hands and knees, or suffered a most frightening paralysis of spirit while struggling to open windows and fling back covers and thus expose to the healthy air outside some bed that one of them had slept in, though it was never mine to know which one — the young mistress or the young master or Mlud or Teddy, had I been so fortunate.

Oppression! Oppression! Could there be still more awaiting the likes of a girl as young as I and a foundling too? There could.

Naturally I had to confess to myself that the pig going so slowly round on its spit above the coals, speaking of snout to tail as I could not help thinking through the clouds of my consternation, was sending forth an aroma that should have put the most timorous girl at ease — but not me. No heavenly scent nor heavenly elixir either could calm my fears that day, and it did not help that the kitchen was unduly hot and the babies more colicky than their wont and Mr. Jakes and Mrs. Grant more pleased with themselves than usual. And especially did it not help that the pig on the spit was so large and infantlike that I could not help seeing the resemblance and then chiding myself for having such crude thoughts, such wicked thoughts, on the very day of my undoing, as I feared it would be.

So the pig changed color from white

to pink and the babies demanded to be attended to, and I sent sprawling from the table a cartload, as it seemed to me, of carrots, and then the same of potatoes, all of which I must retrieve and continue trying to peel but not cut myself. A bleeding finger in the dining hall would not do, as I told myself, thinking my admonitions and trying to quell the shaking that erupted out of myself now here, now there, despite my efforts, remembering that I had not slept the night before, lying in my sweat of fear as fierce as little Martha's fever, and before the first light scrubbing myself from a cold bucket and wishing I had clothes more fit for the occasion, demeaning or not.

More potent and pleasing grew the pig's aroma, golden became its plumpness as Mrs. Grant ladled the poor creature's own melted fat back over its broad tender self, with the little tail tightening and the eye sockets growing emptier and wetter by the moment, and the little teeth increasingly exposed as if that shining animal were grinning at his own plight, as he well might have done. Oh, but I could not grin at mine. And every time Mr. Jakes opened the door into the corridor leading to the dining hall, and I heard their voices, I thought to fall to my knees and cling to a leg of the kitchen table and be done with it. How could I possibly carry that massive pig in to them, as if they were royalty and I their infallible servant? And the pig weighing more than one of Mrs. Grant's babies any day.

Even as I continued to bedevil myself with such worries, which were real enough, poor little Martha was burning up with fever and clinging as best she could to one of my own two legs, so that every now and then I must swoop down and free myself from her little arms, which I did not like to do, while Mrs. Grant glared at my gentleness and I would catch the sound of the young mistress telling one of her foxhunting stories and feel my body drowning inside my clothes and my mouth going dry, I can tell you. How could I do what soon enough I would be told to do? How could I? And no equivocating allowed nor quarter given.

It took both Mrs. Grant and me to carry the spitted pig to the platter and slide him off that spit too hot to touch and onto his great silver bed, which the two of us were forced to do, biting our lips and grunting for the weight of him, while Mr. Jakes was off at the sideboard in the dining hall and opening bottles of claret — claret! whatever that was, but no doubt to match their finery as I thought while struggling with my end of the pig and blowing a damp strand of hair from my eyes.

Mercy, Mother! Spare me!

But the good mother had not been able to help me in the past, nor could she now. For truth to tell when I heard the tinkling that came from the silver bell that sat at the young mistress's elbow, though for the helpless moment I tried to tell myself that it was one of the kitchen bells that was tinkling or perhaps the Angelus bell itself, no matter that inside me I knew the truth, suddenly I felt that I was going not to faint, as might have been expected, but to vomit in the same way as had the young master, and I never having had a drink of whiskey in my young life.

Off with you now. Just put the roast in front of Mlud and serve their plates to their left sides. And quick about it. Don't you hear the young mistress ringing?

Yes, Mum. I hear her ringing.

So there it was at last and unavoidable. So I hefted the platter, my arms spread wide enough for my hands to grip the handles, which by now were almost as hot as the spit had been, and even before reaching the doorway out of the kitchen knew that carrying that platter and its burden was all but beyond my abilities this time, since the platter was twice the size of the tea tray and the pig himself must have doubled his weight in his cooking, no matter that reason said he was surely lighter than before his spitting, because of all the golden fat he had lost.

Again came the sound of the bell, the impatient thing, and off I went, just as I had been bidden, and determined that there was not a pig in any sty in the country round that I could not carry, with all the muscular strength that I had developed on the playing field at Saint Martha's.

Put the platter in front of Mlud, child. There's the dear.

Child? Child? Who in Heaven's name did she think she was, addressing me with that condescension as thick on her voice as lard? And she only two or three years older than I at best.

A little more claret, Mlud? Jakes, please fill Mlud's glass.

No doubt the anger she roused in me and the fact of Mr. Jakes's presence, despite my antipathy for his walleye and wen and not having forgiven him for having so rudely snatched me up that day in the past, gave me the strength I needed to avoid disgrace. So I turned round, for I had backed my way through the doorway connecting the corridor to the dining hall, and saw the musty eyes and antlers of all the deer heads mounted round the four walls of that large formal room, and smelled the savory aroma of the roast I demanded of myself to carry, and in a glance saw the young mistress smiling from the far end of the table and in the middle on the opposite side from me the young master just reaching out for his claret and, his back to me, Mlud, as he had to be, facing the young mistress with his head in bandages.

I staggered once, staggered twice at the sight of those bandages, I can tell you, but then quickly found the explanation — foxhunting, Dervla! What else? — and thus regained my balance and my determination too as I took the final step to the table and felt the deer's eyes staring down at me in pity or encouragement, I could not tell which.

Pity, of course.

For then, having gotten as far as the old man's elbow, I swung round boldly and, as anyone would have known except my own poor self covered in sweat and not much more than some witless thing, came face-to-face with Teddy. Yes, Teddy himself! And in this terrible moment I saw a total lack of recognition in the eyes that were as soft and blind as all the dead eyes of the deer adorning the walls above our heads. Oh Mother of us all as we are taught, he did not recognize his Dervla!

So I dropped the pig, as was to be expected.

Cried out, I say, and in one thoughtless gasp allowed the platter to tilt and the wretched pig in his shrouds and veils of parsley to go diving straight to the floor with a naked thud as deep and resounding as any blow I ever struck on my bass drum, and slide a few feet and lie there grinning up at me, his four fat little legs tucked close to his belly and his four hoofs shiny black and sparkling.

Mercy, Mother! Spare me!

No doubt from the smell that issued from the pig and filled the room like a gas, I must have been grinning as cruelly as that creature lying there in mockery I would never in my life live down. The young mistress began to speak, thought better of it and took a sip of wine. The young master leaned forward as if we must needs have a repetition of the episode of the boot, though there was no boot in sight. Teddy looked sweetly at the pig on the floor as he had when looking into his own Dervla's face now as red as the claret and wet with the few tears I could not hold back. As for Mr. Jakes, there he stood, bottle in hand and bloody towel over his arm, making no move to assist me or to whisper encouragement either.

Curtain upon curtain of blackness fell, all avenues were blocked by felled trees behind which lurked men in black and wearing masks, until I shuddered and came to my senses, knowing that I had only myself to thank for the shame I had incurred and for the grim humor enlivening the pig on the floor, and knowing as I had known before that there was no one but myself to help me, not even the sacred Mother I had appealed to, since of course she could not intervene except in matters regarding turmoils of the soul, or its splendors, and there were those who questioned even these.

So there in the completeness of my humiliation I stooped down. Reached out my hands. Stepped closer to the pig. Forced myself to descend to hands and knees. Bit my top lip and then my lower. Squeezed shut my eyes. Held my breath. And then glory be and so forth, caught hold of the pig. Just so. Tried to grip in my hands that slippery beast.

While in the silence they surely could not have been so unchristian as to maintain deliberately, though they did so anyway, they watched. The young mistress. The young master. Mr. Jakes. Mlud, who was my own Teddy no matter what they called him or why. Until I began to grapple with that pig, and the young mistress, apparently unable to bear any longer the pain they were inflicting on a young girl, Irish or not, suddenly spoke up.

Jakes! Whiskey!

Down there on my hands and knees I knew that along with everything else I was driving them to drink, as if they were as Irish as anyone, though they were not, and I myself despicable in my pathetic state. I saw the black-trousered legs of Mr. Jakes gliding past me in the fading light, I reached again for the pig who again eluded me, even as I clung to the tip of an ear, and slid round and round me in a circle until I caught the tail and heard the creature squeal, which he could not have done, and drew him to me, slimy and hot as he was yet from the coals. Oh, there was nothing for it but to haul him onto the slant of my knees and to grip him top and bottom as I would a rebellious child, and I did so and lifted him as high as my chest all covered by this time with the slime of his golden skin. And stood up, tottering. And with my own hands returned him to the platter, for which they might have thanked me or sighed in unison, as I thought as inadvertently I wiped the sweat from my face and thereby smeared my face with the grease of the pig who was lying askew on the platter feet up instead of on his stomach with his feet tucked tidily underneath. On the platter exactly as he had been on the floor, as they deserved, I thought, and stumbled like the light from that cold room.

To my own room, to which I climbed immediately, and shed my clothes and with them did my best to wipe myself clean, and then donned the nightdress and took to my bed, feeling the heat of my shame increasing hourly into little Martha's fever, or the same, as I finally knew it to be in the dark of night.

Awake. Feverish. But not so feverish as to disregard what I knew to be the moral truth of the thing. I must brave the dogs. Nothing less than braving the dogs would do. That very night. That very hour. I could wait no longer. Even as I extricated my burning self from my hot sheets and blankets, and caught the lingering scent of roasted pork, I knew that I must find my Teddy that selfsame night, torn to shreds though I might be for my efforts.

Pitter pitter pitter pitter and more of the same, which might have been the sound of my naked feet along those corridors and up the grand

236

sweeping staircase if you please, as if I were a new arrival from across the seas and come to spend a month or so in all her glory, jokes at the expense of my own countrymen included, such as *Who was in the bed, Paddy,* as I once heard the young mistress say, except that I made not a sound as I progressed in eerie confidence down those same corridors and up that same sweeping staircase, more like a night visitant and all but invisible at that, than any guest the young mistress might welcome into her open arms. No one ever used the front staircase with its curving balustrade as wide or wider than my stone bridge and its rotted wall hangings and dust so thick I should have been ashamed of myself. I don't know why that night I chose to ascend in fullest view of whatever or whoever awaited me at the top, but so I did, naked except for my night-dress that had been absorbing the sweat of my fever so that to Mr. Jakes, for instance, I would have looked quite naked and then some, had he been awaiting me in the darkness at the top of the stair, which he was not. Up there the night inside the old house was packed so thick and still that I could not see a thing, though thanks to all my reluctant exploring in response to the bells I knew exactly where I was, without so much as a pause or pursing of my lips dry and cracking with the fever while the rest of me was sweating out the same. Oh yes, knew where I was and no mistake about that either, which was exactly where I was not allowed unless sum-moned, as I had never been and the better for that too, as I told myself going forward toward the master bedroom, which in fact and as I say I had never seen from within, Mrs. Grant doing the maid's work in that room, as she told me herself, and the chamber pot always just outside the door expecting me.

Dogs? Where are you, dogs?

I suppose it was only thanks to the fever that I had courage enough to proceed directly into the jaws of the dogs, as I might say, except that I neither heard nor saw a sign of them the entire night, as if that night the maliciousness in which they slept was too profound to suffer disturbing by a girl as inconsequential as I and clothed only in her young mistress's discarded nightgown, in which I might as well have been naked, as I have said. Or had the young mistress called them off?

Where are you, dogs?

Of course I would hardly have known it had they pounced on me, three or four animals as tall as I and heavier, bounding with one mind onto the hapless intruder and tearing her apart and to pieces swiftly, savagely, and in silence despite the barking and growling that accompanies the rabid concentration of dogs kept in a house, at least in a house as large and humanly impoverished as Great Manor. And not a sound from me either, I can tell you that. No scream of pain, no cry for help, not that there was a soul in the place who would have heard my shrieks and come running. Only the teeth and the gnashing and their great hairless bodies, or nearly so, and hotter than mine, that's for sure, and making short work of me with nothing left but the shreds of the ravished nightgown and some splattered blood.

Dogs? Dogs?

Was I fool enough to be whispering to my own attackers as they might have been, to be calling them forth when in fact I was so near delirium that I cared not a farthing for the terror that was helping to fuel the very fever in which I was consumed? I was. I was as I would have told my confessor had I but had the chance to kneel at his little window, as I had not. Better to get it over beforehand though I wanted nothing more than to be spared that swift but terrible end like the poor little wild animal smothered and devoured too by a pack of massive hounds coming from nowhere and afterwards loping away and showing in their slimy chops clear evidence of what they had done, had anyone cared to look. Like the scraps of my night-gown, though subtler.

Where are you, dogs?

And was I the greater fool to be entering, and in the dead of night, the very room forbidden me by Mrs. Grant, and like the silly wraith I was, to be walking straight to the majestic bed, sagging canopy and all, that was the largest of the bulky shapes that filled that room as I could but dimly see? I was. Without hesitation and with no concern for the feelings of Teddy, who might have been lying in that bed that loomed as big as a boat with the young mistress dozing beside him for all I knew. Exactly. So was I handing over my wits to my delirium like coins to the pauper? Or abandoning my sense of purpose to the total lack of reason that pervaded that household? Not at all. And quite the opposite. For within the hottest depths of my ever-increasing fever surely I had found my own clear pool of reason and meant to pit my reason against the unreason with which I was surrounded all the day long and the night too, especially this one. For if my object was to find Teddy and carry him off with me then and there, this night, and if the young mistress had determined to call my Teddy Mlud and to treat him as such, then if one thing followed another as of course it did not, where else would I look for Mlud if not in the master bedroom? But as for catching the two of them together, and suffering embarrassment as great as my fear of the dogs, which I was more than willing to do as I have already said, my alternative powers of reasoning told me even then that I was probably running little risk of doing so, for would it have made much sense for the young mistress to share the bed that rose before me with her own daddo? Though of course he was not her daddo, as at least I knew, fever or no fever, and in fact was nobody's daddo like the rest of them and as any foundling girl can attest. No daddo, no mummy. So I was no fool to be entering that room.

Who was in the bed, Paddy?

I stopped. Swayed. Faltered. The bed was not an arm's length from where I stood and was only a denser mass of blackness in a chamber devoid of light and admitting no light since the drapes were tightly drawn and had in fact hung that way, closed to light, since the very hour that some old gent, Mlud of a former time as I supposed, had ceased to be. There I was and there was the bed, with its sagging canopy in a chamber larger than any other in Great Manor and dustier too, which made me think that either Mrs. Grant was not telling me the truth about cleaning it herself or simply that she had no talent for the work of a maid, having been raised to the kitchen. Whereupon I thought of the chamber pot and heard a rustling from within that enormous bed and felt my understanding struck another terrible blow as with a cold hammer, say, and felt my entire self turn cold.

Who was in the bed, Paddy?

But the joke was on the jokers, surely, and suddenly and no matter

the state of my reason or understanding either, I knew that there was
no salvation for me except in that
great bed despite the other occupants
who might or might not be sleeping
peacefully or otherwise therein. I
longed to lie in it, to burrow down, to
hide beneath the silk and woolen bedding with which that ancient piece of
furniture was heaped, as my sensitive
sense of smell told me it was through
the ice and fire of which I myself was
the source, and grow warm or freeze
in oblivion at least. In that great bed.

Oh, and then the rustling sounds
were in the bed and so too was I, just
as I had known I must be if I was not
to drop to the floor. But there was no
dropping to the floor for me, though
I had not the slightest notion how I
came to be lying beneath the sheets

and blankets and quilts with my head on one of the several or more bolsters, but there it was. I awoke to being in that bed, that is, and dared not move hand or limb for fear of touching someone else's. Teddy's most of all since I knew in my delirium that I was too done in for rescuing, until the fever passed, that is, though it did occur to me that had his fingers crept into mine as a sign of his existence only, say, it would have been reassuring. But then I dropped off. I heard nothing and felt myself as rigid as a mouse but on fire, of course, and freezing, and it was in the midst of such sensations that may have been only indications of who knows what deadly illness, that the old horse belonging to Evelyn Stack's father came to me as clearly as the water in my pool of reason. There he stood, as actual as the hunting saddle that I had seen straddling the bottom of the sweeping balustrade on my way up, though at the time I had not cared to comment to myself on that saddle, the sight of it until now obliterated by my preoccupation.

Furthermore, in my first full loss of consciousness as it must have been, the presence of that grieving horse did not entangle me as on former days in questions concerning the reality of figments, or lies as Teddy would have said straight-out had he been with me and up to talking, but simply enabled me to know all at once that in my case love and grief were indistinguishable, which was not such a bad thing after all. And the saddle on the balustrade? Long abandoned and dried out like

248

me and no doubt smelling like the boot in the parlor before the young master got hold of it.

When I drifted back into wakefulness, for such I did and with only the mildest surprise, for dream or oblivion or wakefulness were all the same to me in my fever, when my recovery was nip and tuck as I understood toward the end, I heard the rustling sound again and, parched with thirst though I was and thinking I could not last for long in this condition, tossing and moaning as I was confident I had been doing, I listened as hard as I could to that rustling. For now, as I heard, that sound was accompanied by another. Squealing. Tiny sounds of squealing. The tiniest sounds of pleasure that might have come from pinching, say, or poking.

Who was in the bed, Paddy?

Still I did not allow myself to move. I dared not. For reasons already stated, valid or not. Yet even without so much as a foot or finger, doing my best to avoid what would have pleased my mounting ardor but not my reasoning of the thing so far, my bodily senses told me that the bed was huge, larger than I thought when merely standing beside it, and that it was filled with the same dust that filled the room itself. The feathers within the bolsters were halfway gone to dust, as was the very cloth of the sheets, the wool of the blankets, the silken stuff of the quilts. Oh, time had been passing in that bed whose majesty was equaled only by its history even without the old gent to do his snoring and who knew what else in that dead bed.

Which is when it occurred to me that who or what is dead and gone is not so in truth but only in a continuous state of dying, unless we are speaking of the headstones behind the village church, which is another thing altogether.

But how did I know about that canopy overhead? If the room was as tightly sealed as I had thought? And the door so firmly closed day and night? Why, simply because the drapes were not as bitterly drawn as they had seemed to me, and the room not totally dark, as I had thought, so that it was not unreasonable to see the canopy and at the same time to suffer the old gent's night of nights, or his last, that is, though presumably he saw nothing at all when that night fell. Canopy or no canopy, there was no

251

denying the size of the bed so that three of us could have lain abreast therein with one of us, myself, totally unaware of the others — unless she moved. And I was bound and determined not to move. And there was no denying the weight and vastness of the bedding in which I hid with my heart thumping and my ears attuned, listening, that is, to the squealing, also undeniable and so provocative that it might have been coming from behind a closet door closed on darkness and whoever might have been hiding inside, old or young and beginning to do what Micka had been describing to me in the barn.

When I came to my senses, hotter than ever and feeling that my very person had become illicit though I was still not attuned to specifics, the squealing sounds were louder and in the darkness had assumed a color. Pink. And seeing that pink suffusion and hearing those sounds of squealing, what did I do? I squirmed. I began to squirm, despite myself, as if the squealing had gotten inside my own body and the wet pink color had become mine too, as no doubt it had. Oh, I was not thrashing about, as I might have been had I lost my self-control altogether. And my squirming was not what anyone might have called pronounced. I was not squirming so visibly or obviously, that is, as to offend our own Foundling Mother had she come upon me squirming and squealing in the night when the other girls were asleep and behaving themselves. But squirming I was and continued to do so even after dropping off, which I could not help but do.

Then I awoke. Abruptly. With a difference, which is understating the thing entirely. For lying there in the nest I had drenched, in the bed I had kept myself from exploring, I felt a hand upon me. Not mine. Somebody else's. A human hand for sure. Resting upon me. Ready to move.

Which naturally caused me to hold my breath and to stop my squirming, or to so attempt with whatever degree of success I could not know, though at least I was doing my best in the area of self-restraint in the firm belief that effacing myself might cause the effacement of that heavy hand as well, which proved untrue but gave me an interim in which to know that the hand upon me was too large and weighty to be Teddy's, a realization that brought me relief and disappointment in a single stroke but was of course no help in ruling out the young master or Mr. Jakes or helping me to decide between the two.

Then I awoke.

I was not squirming. There was not a breath of life inside me. The wiggling inside my mind, for such it had been, had certainly given way to thinking, and yet I had been so successful at holding down all my sensations, good and bad, prohibited or encouraged as I thought they might have been in that decaying bed, that of course I had made myself quite unaware of the invasive hand that had for some time been moving upon me, as a matter of fact, but only to wipe my face and to carry the strands of damp hair from off my brow. Whereupon I felt myself smiling and going under again, without the slightest resistance to what was happening and exactly as I heard the two voices at my bedside and recognized them and so knew that at least I did not have to contend with the presence of the young master in my condition, so that my decency, as certainly I thought of it, was left intact.

I was awake. I was not squirming. I was alone in the old gent's bed as I saw at a glance since the tall drapes had been drawn somewhat apart so as to admit a minimum of daylight but not too much. I was alone in the room too, the young mistress and Mr. Jakes, who had surely been discussing how sick I was in my oblivion, having set off, apparently, for whatever might be required for tending the distressingly ill, for such I knew I was in this moment of clarity briefer but also more lucid than those that had come to me so far. For instance, and as I could see perfectly well and hence knew full well, on the opposite wall in the shadows were portraits of the old gent, or his predecessor, and an elderly woman in a wig, the two of them staring back at me from across the room as if to make me more than ever aware of my disheveled condition and the guilt such a condition should ordinarily entail. The point being that I had kicked myself free of the covers and so thrashed about that my nighty, as we used to call that garment at Saint Martha's, was twisted up beneath my armpits, as it seemed to me, and threatening for sure my decency which, I confess, had suddenly faded to but a dim concept in that warm light. There I was, innocently exposed, and exhausted, and blinking my wide-open eyes which all at once took in everything. The portraits across the way. The bed quite empty except for me, as I saw by turning my poor head side to side, which did not convince me that I had been alone in the bed this entire time, however long it might have been. And listening, no matter how I moved my head. Sharply, despite my wet hair and face and body and nighty too. Listening with great attentiveness. For the squealing was back. Clearly enough. And in the bed too. With me. But somewhere toward the foot of the bed as my hearing told me and as until this very moment I had not known. I waited, listening to those tiny sounds, and then, and despite my weakness, for I had all but worn myself out with the tossing and turning, when I was not oblivious or briefly awake, that is, I raised myself on an elbow and bent my head and took a good long look. And smiled.

Mice.

A colony of the little creatures, as it seemed to me, and all of them pink and naked as only newborn mice can be and with their eyes still sealed shut yet bulging. An army of them as I thought, a fat nest of them, blindly crawling and moiling and rolling upon each other and tumbling off, with heads as long as their bodies and legs so undeveloped as to be incapable of propelling them at all, as it appeared to me. Yet there they were — a bare brood of mice as I thought with a nod to Mrs. Grant, and squirming about as slowly as the flesh crawls. And squealing. And squeaking, the lascivious things, and not even able to feed themselves as yet.

But my own flesh, to pursue the figure, was not crawling, I can attest to that, and the girlish scream that might have burst from any other Irish girl did not burst from me, for at the certain sight of the little nuzzling things in all their nudity, suddenly I could only think of the horror that that heap of mice in his bed would surely have inspired in the old gent, and quickly too, with all the shouts and bell ringing that would have attended his discovery — which, along with the likelihood that in but a moment or two I should feel the first of them against my bare foot, foot and unformed mice being that close together, set me to smiling again and falling back and slipping off as into my last coma, but willingly so.

. . . and you shall have to make her decent, Jakes.

. . . Happily, Miss.

. . . and keep her warm while bringing down the fever.

. . . Exactly, Miss.

The old gent's room grew darker, then brighter, as the pink suffusion all about me intensified and then disappeared and then gradually returned, and deeper down I sank, no matter the size of the arms that embraced me and lifted me and pulled down my nighty and raised to my whitened lips the cup.

. . . Oh, look there, Jakes. She has done it again.

. . . At least she doesn't know what's

happening, Miss.

. . . At least she couldn't have better care than yours.

The hotter my body the colder the icy cloth on my head. My ears were plugged with the sediment that had stopped up my nose, and through the pain in my ears I heard them talking, occasionally, and every now and then, conscious of the rawness between my upper lip and the tip of my nose, I felt his big hand as a pillow raising my head and holding it steady while happily enough I sipped the medicinal stuff in the cup.

. . . How does she feel, Jakes?

. . . Very warm, Miss.

. . . Top to bottom?

. . . Top to bottom, Miss.

. . . Do you know, Jakes, you may be the only mother the poor child has ever had.

. . . Safe to say. And I am your own mother as well, Miss.

. . . But how pleasant it is that Father has come back to us. For good.

For all of it I could feel my own worsening while they talked. Let them hover about me and administer the ice and medicinal fluids and keep me packed in the blankets and every now and then fluff up the bolsters that split at the seams and leaked dust and feathers into the old gent's bed on which I too might breathe my last, for the breath in my chest was growing more labored and thickening, and my fever rising. But all the while that they busied themselves about me, and nursed me, and in solemn silence looked at what they could see of my poor flushed body bare as a bone, I knew that I was smiling and had nothing to fear, thanks mainly to the secret I had managed to keep concealed at the foot of the bed, no matter that I kept kicking off the covers whenever I could. Even when I heard the two of them discussing Mrs. Grant and the old woman's claim that the fever I had come down with had finally infected little Martha and been all but the death of her, when I knew full well that it was the other way round, I could only smile to myself at the injustice and sink a bit deeper into the ache in my bones. The sicker I grew the safer I was, as I knew by the rattling in my scummy chest, and not because I was resorting to silent prayers either, for I had already learned my lesson regarding prayers.

They drew open the drapes that hung as stiffly as dead skin, and closed them again. They lit a candle at my bedside and blew it out. They debated sending for Dr. Somebody-or-other who must have attended Teddy as I told myself despite my pain and shallow breath, but decided to rely on Mr. Jakes and the experience he had had with sick children for all his life in service, including of course the young mistress. I coughed, I dripped, I strove to hear the sounds of the infant mice all but drowned out in my coughing and the endless talking.

. . . You'd best listen to her chest, Jakes. She sounds worse to me.

. . . She is, Miss.

At which my eyes popped open, you may be sure. Or partially so at least. Clarity returned. Rain was falling, as I could hear through the open drapes. And there, sitting on the edge of the old gent's bed with his coat removed and his shirtsleeves rolled, was Mr. Jakes, and the young mistress a step or two behind him and then leaning over his shoulder — she did that! — not with concern for my welfare but the keenest possible interest in something else. Then she whispered into her butler's ear, which might as well have been mine so clearly did I hear the words.

. . . Listen to her chest, Jakes.

Which as I say I heard as clearly as if my ears had not been ringing, though it was only a whisper. As for Mr. Jakes, he was frowning as deeply as if he had been a country doctor when in fact he was only a butler with a walleye and a wen on his neck.

Wen on his neck! . . .

Which nearly did me in, I can tell you. For what could he possibly mean to do if not rest his wen upon my all but naked chest as I clearly saw through my half-open eyes. *Wen on his neck!* . . . And oh, that wen was as large as little Martha's fist and as hairy as some small headless animal that would have set even Mrs. Grant to screaming had she found it lying in a dish on the kitchen table, no matter her warts and imperturbable nature. And hadn't I once been as revolted by Mr. Jakes's hairy abnormality as by the white of his terrible eye? I had indeed, as I dimly remembered through the safety of my influenza, as they said it was, and watching as Mr. Jakes leaned over me, came closer, and slowly allowed his head and neck and wen, now glowing green as some thorny sea creature crying out for water, to lie upon me. Oh, it lay quietly upon me, that glowing wen that was surely readying itself to move. Now, however, as I had known the while, I was not the least repelled by the weight of the old butler's head on my chest or the sensation of his ear against me or the touch of his hairy wen from which it did not occur to me to flinch, though under earlier circumstances I might have thought that I could not bear for a moment the feel of the thing crawling across my ribs and bosom. But not now. Even as I paid as close attention as I could to the weight of his shaggy head rising and falling with the sloshing sound of my own breath, I knew that the butler's wen was of no concern to me one way or another and that my decency was as safely mine as his wen was his, no matter the actual reason he was moving his head around my chest and listening. But of course this portion of his medical examination, for all the pleasure I took to be basking in it and whether it was fraught with moral implications or not, was abruptly ended by the young mistress's sharp cry.

Jakes! Look there! Oh, throw them out, the horrible little creatures!

Yes, Miss! I shall do so, Miss. At once!

Which in fact ended all further care and examinations I might have received at the hands of Mr. Jakes, though I was yet far from well. But at least she did not scream. I had to give her that.

Up with ya! Up ya get! And quick about it!

It was a sharp little whisper yet quite

as fierce as the skinny thumb and fore-finger gripping my wrist like a bracelet of cold bone. At the sound of such peremptory urging and the sudden pain of his grip on my wrist, I came awake quite as if I had never been lying in my drowsy coma in the first place nor ever been cared for by the two of them. Cured, I knew, in the instant I saw Micka crouching at my bedside with his unruly hair and tight fearful angry face and his whispering and seizing hold of my wrist. Cured for sure, as if I had not been stricken near dead like a child and as clear in my head now as Micka, who was in a terrible hurry to do me some wonder-ful good as was plain to see by the milky angry look in his eye.

Oh, I obeyed all right and without a moment's hesitation or even a thought to my decency as I donned the shirt and breeches, with him looking on, mind you, and then snatching hold of my wrist again and starting off at such a secret silent rapid pace that he might have been some ragged fairy flying.

The grand staircase. The saddle for which there was no horse. The ballroom as broad as a battlefield and empty of everyone, past and present and future, save Micka and me. A French door standing ajar with teeth of broken glass still caught in the casement. Micka was the first out, turning himself sideways and over his shoulder bidding me to do the same, and to step carefully, as I did except that as I might have known I ripped a good and proper tear in my breeches on one of those snags of broken glass exactly when from behind me, from far in the depths of the place where Mrs. Grant was no doubt lording it over the kitchen, there came the faintest violent ringing of a bell — that would not be answered! Ever! At least by me. And if not by me, then whom? Ring on, I cried to myself. Ring on to your heart's content!

Then I unplucked myself from the snags of glass and stepped to my freedom. Outside. And began at once to purify my recently recovered lungs with Irish air and feeling the circlet of Micka's thumb and forefinger still locked on my wrist.

Down we went, off we went, the two of us slithering as one from tree to tree and bush to bush, in all the speed and stealth we could manage, first in the direction of the stables and afterwards in quite another, as I must wait and see. I did not look back but crouched and ran, as indeed I could not help but do with Micka pulling me along as he was.

First meet of the season.

Which was his only comment and only explanation, which made me think that we should see the stableyard filled with the same horses and riders and dogs I had seen when my own Teddy had been run down by the lot of them. Neighboring horses, that is, and neighboring riders astride and sidesaddle, carrying their whips and dented horns, with the sunlight shining off their top hats and off their hearty voices too, and five score dogs milling about under the horses' feet and squealing even when they had not been stepped on, as they deserved to be. But when we peered into that frosty stableyard from our secret vantage point behind a shed, what did I see but only the two of them, the young mistress mounted on her favorite horse, the same as had caused us all this trouble in the first place, and Teddy sitting as proud as you please on a great black snorting thing whose eye, as I could see even from that distance, was rolling about with all the anger that that ugly beast could but contain.

And poor Teddy dressed in an ancient hunting costume that the young mistress must have unearthed at the height of my fever. Teddy, who did not even know who he was or where except on a horse, and an exceptional old horse too, and proud of being up there though he did not know why, even with the cuffs of his pink coat rolled and the boots that would have slipped off his little feet and calves had it not been for the irons, as I knew from Mr. Lackey that they were called. Thus and so as Teddy would have said. By which I mean that it was still my fate to bear the humiliation that was rightly his, quite as if I was yet enmeshed in the wisps and tangles of the dark pall cast upon me by Great Manor, though I was free of the place as I well knew.

Hardly had the two of them turned their backs to us and started out of the stableyard and down the lane, the young mistress laughing for our benefit as I would have thought had she known of our spying, and poor Teddy looking lost and foolish in the old gent's clothes. Then Micka gave me a yank as if I might have been recalcitrant and not the responsive creature he must have known I was, and pulled me after him at a goodly clip, I can tell you, but in the opposite direction from that chosen by the riders I had thought he had meant to follow.

There we were, stooped over and running at top speed, and me just out of sickbed too, no matter that I was cured and just in time too. For the longest while there was nothing to hear but the sound of Micka's breath and mine, such as it was, along with the snapping twigs and branches and the fleetest sound of our footfalls as we hid ourselves like pale birds across barren fields and other such open and empty places. Oh, weren't we bent close to the earth even when we found our way through stands of dismal trees and skirted bogs and marshes and rushed headlong into blinding remnants of the fog as yet unrisen. Down hairy banks and into slurry ditches we went with nothing to throw us off our steadfast track except the occasional covey of one kind of wild bird or another that rose from under our very feet with a dreadful sound as of wooden hands clapping back there in the empty chapel. Had it not been for Micka's purpose, which I could not deny or fail to trust, I would have thought that this flight of ours was cruel and random and without sense, except that I could not help myself and understood, though I did not know how, that Micka was subjecting himself and specially me to such an arduous ordeal because he was trying to outrun the hunt, or something that momentous.

Outrun the hunt! Which is exactly how it came to me as suddenly I heard the far-off sound of horses and rushing hounds, and a single blast on a horn as frail as thread, and suddenly understood that the hunt was strung out in a long thin line that could not fail to cross our own! To bisect our own! Or to put it the other way round, which was more appropriate to Micka's plan, for plan he had like some clever animal in its last fever of duress, our own path, if we but followed it as we could not help but do, would soon enough intersect the path of the hunt! Inevitably! Though not exactly, as I soon discovered.

Then we lost them. Then they reappeared, veering this way and that but out of the silence suddenly finding again the long straight thin line I had detected. Ravishing the very air, I thought, in the interim of silence that left my Irish air in peace.

Then they returned. The sounds of them. Riders. Horses. Hounds. Approaching though from still another direction as it seemed to me.

Then Micka flung himself forward and facedown and me with him, of course, at the edge of the largest bank of all as the clamor I had expected to burst upon us once more ceased altogether and in its wake left only the deadliest silence I had ever heard. There we lay side by side, torn and gasping. And the silence worse than the deafening I suffered the day I cut the young mistress's hair or went my solitary way in my fever. Had the hunt again lost its own direction? Was it gone? Exactly so, as it came to me, except for one of its members. But one, as I heard by the sound of approaching hooves, and no more. A single rider who for whatever reason or none at all had broken away from the rest of them. And in a slow and heavy gallop was coming toward Micka and me as if that rider could see us lying in the way and would run us down. Trample us underfoot.

The young mistress! How like her to find me even where I could not be found and send me back to Great Manor, and Micka too with his little tail hanging. After all this and all the way we had come.

Oh, but it was disloyal of me to think such ignoble thoughts of Micka, for that approaching rider could not see the empty air ahead and certainly could not see such a miserable pair as

Micka and me lying in wait for trampling or crunching or whatever it was to be. Because the embankment at the foot of which we lay was as tall as the trees and, where it faced us, was cut in a terrible perpendicular. And the rider astride that galloping horse was somewhere atop the embankment and could not even know of its falling off, let alone see the prospective victims lying helplessly below.

Cover your head! Don't look!

But of course I did no such thing and as soon as the galloping stopped and all the air that high above was filled with the horse so large as to obscure the black sky overhead and even the faintest light of the sun, the poor thing as big as some unnatural bird, though it had no wings, worse luck for that horse, suspended up

281

there in empty space and with no warning either, I knew that it was not the young mistress after all, since viewed even from its underside, as I was viewing it, the color of that poor beast was black.

Oh, what a crash was the terrible crash that followed! The boulders flew about and landed, the haunches and neck and tail all landed separately, as it seemed to me, and the legs and hooves too, crumpling and breaking while from the depths of that black horse there came one compelling sound to announce once and for all the breaking of its wretched neck. Once and for all, while the earth shook and one of its mad eyes caught my own. As for the rider, oh, hadn't he been flung a goodly distance, yet had fared no better than the horse, lying in his own small crumpled heap and with his own neck broken as I recognized at once though ignorant as I was of the surgeon's lore. At least I reached him swiftly enough, in a few desperate bounds, and cradled him against me, the head and broken neck, that is, to hear his final words so tender with love and intelligence in contrast to the bellow that had come from the black horse that had killed him.

Dervla! Yourself, my dear! I must have known all the time that you'd be expecting me, though it took this little knock on the head to return me to love and recognition.

So it had.

Off with ya! And quick about it. We're going to torch Great Manor tonight!

And him no more than a boy to be talking thus!

When at last I reached the edge of Carrickfergus, which of course I did and without Micka too, and though the road to Carrickfergus was crooked enough to mislead many a traveler warier than I, I saw the spires rising and above the noise of the city heard the distant shouting of the boys in their field.

I had planned the while to make my way directly to Saint Martha's. But then, with passersby giving me odd looks and no wonder too, I thought of Teddy, with his face like the face of an insect even without his respirator, though I loved him the same, and changed my course and went directly to Canty's Pub. And this time, when I entered alone and like something the dog might have dragged inside, Michael Canty himself came quickly enough from behind the bar and without so much as a word of welcome, but giving me his hands and eyes and smell of him too, led me through the fellows sitting round with their caps on the backs of their heads and their smiles as pretty as anything I had seen since poor Teddy's death, and who out of courtesy to me kept talking.

I need not have had any misgiving, as I had had though for a moment only, since in the back room Michael Canty did not even think of asking my age.

The same green log was burning in Canty's Pub. Outside, the air of Carrickfergus was thick with the shouting of the boys and the sound of my drum, as beaten by another girl of course.

When at last I stood on the steps of Saint Martha's, waiting for the door to open, I had already prepared to ask Mrs. Jencks for my letters, first thing. And yes it was Mrs. Jencks, indeed, who hugged me as properly as Mrs. Jennings would have done, and yes she gave me my packet of letters tied up with a green ribbon if you please. Which is how I came to know who I am.

And who is that?

Foundling Mother, of course, as I had known my life long that I would be. Mother of not a single one of my own, as I had known it would be from the start, but mother of thirty or so girls at a time, which is the same thing.

So now it is I who tell them stories. And who reassures them when they don't know who they are or why. I who stand singing at the end of the dark room where all my foundling girls lie sleeping.

The employees of G.K. Hall hope you have enjoyed this Large Print book. All our Large Print titles are designed for easy reading, and all our books are made to last. Other G.K. Hall books are available at your library, through selected bookstores, or directly from us.

For information about titles, please call:

(800) 257-5157

To share your comments, please write:

Publisher
G.K. Hall & Co.
P.O. Box 159
Thorndike, ME 04986